IN THE DRAGON'S LAIR

CHARLES RAY

North Potomac, MD

ISBN: 0615847277
ISBN-13: 978-0615847276 (Uhuru Press)

DEDICATION

To the men and women of the U.S. Foreign Service, and the employees at the U.S. Department of State. Even though few Americans know it, these people contribute as much to our country's national security as every tank, ship, or airplane, often with fewer resources, and always without fanfare. Only noticed when things go wrong, they nonetheless continue to give of their time and talents for the benefit of their fellow citizens.

ACKNOWLEDGMENTS

The number of people to whom I owe a debt of gratitude for inspiring this book are too many to list here. Those senior colleagues I met when I first joined the Foreign Service in 1982 gave me some idea of what it was like in 1975, when I, as a member of the US Army, knew as little about it as other Americans. My decades in the bureaucracy, though, have given me a definite slant on that peculiar institution, which I'm sure comes through in the story. While this is a work of fiction, and is not meant to represent any individuals or events, I've made every effort, however, to keep the history accurate.

Chapter One

Tuesday, June 24, 1975, Dagastan, Central Asia

A month had passed since the overthrow of Dmitri Kovasc, First Secretary of the Dagastan Communist Party and head of state, and his replacement by Milosevic Dragov, the deputy head of Dagastan's security services. Merely a month since the chaotic events leading to the death of American ambassador Robert Ellingsworth, and David Morgan, Ellingsworth's deputy chief of mission (DCM); the number two man in the embassy, was still *charge d'affaires, a.i.,* an archaic French diplomatic term that essentially meant, the one in temporary charge of the embassy's affairs until a suitable replacement could be found.

Morgan didn't find the delay in naming a new ambassador all that strange, as unsettling as it was to him personally. Washington had been caught sleeping by the rapid pace of

1

events in Dagastan, and the system, slow at the best of times, had yet to find someone, prepare his nomination packet, and submit it to the U.S. Senate for the confirmation process, a process that could, depending on the individual, and the mood of Congress at the time, take months.

It had been six months between the time Morgan's first ambassador, Eloise Tarkington, departed Dagastan and Ellingsworth had arrived, despite his name having been put into the hat a full year before her planned departure. During that six month stint in charge, Morgan hadn't made any significant changes in the way the embassy operated because Tarkington had been a people-oriented leader who always took into account the way her actions affected others. Despite his not putting his own personal stamp on the place during his time as boss, Morgan suspected that Ellingsworth had resented him just for *being* in charge. Challenging some of the man's more egregious traits, as Morgan had done on one or two occasions, had only made matters worse.

The deterioration of their relationship culminated in the unfortunate incident when Ellingsworth had invited Morgan to a late-night meeting in a seedy part of Dagastan's capital city, Kazbektun, where they'd been ambushed, and Ellingsworth had been killed by a stray bullet. Morgan couldn't prove anything, but he and the embassy Regional Security Officer

(RSO) Pete Jeffers had been convinced that Ellingsworth had arranged the ambush to get rid of them because they were too close to discovering what he'd been up to in his secretive meetings with Milosevic Dragov, former deputy head of Dagastan's security services, and now the country's leader after he'd led a coup that deposed his former boss, Dmitri Kovasc, the former First Secretary of the Central Committee of Dagastan's Communist Party.

Morgan hadn't communicated his suspicions to Washington, and he'd convinced Jeffers to hold off as well. In the first place, they had no proof. Secondly, he didn't want to smear the name of a Foreign Service colleague without absolute proof of his guilt.

Unlike his first time at the helm, this time, Morgan had made some immediate changes. For starters, his weekly country team meetings, now held every Monday morning at eight sharp, started on time, because he didn't keep people waiting. He also sat at the chair nearest the door, rather than parading the length of the room as Ellingsworth had done; nor did he insist that everyone stand when he entered the room. More often than not, he'd already be in the conference room waiting for the staff when they arrived. He also now included the RSO in all country team meetings, and from time to time, had one of the junior officers from other sections or agencies attend the meetings to act as a note taker. He felt that this was a valuable way to make them feel like an important of the mission's operations, and gave them a sense of what it would be like as they advanced in grade in the service.

He'd designated the political counselor, Dennis Larson, the acting DCM. Larson had moved his number two, a young grade three officer named Joseph Moon, up to be interim head of the political section.

Country team meetings were now livelier; not rowdy, but people no longer felt constrained as they had under Ellingsworth's dictatorial hand. Morgan let the heads of section speak first, only interjecting to ask questions if he didn't fully understand something, and said very little at the end beyond brief instructions for the coming week, or synopses of news he'd heard from Washington through his private channels.

The mood in the embassy was definitely better. So, why, David Morgan wondered, as he sat alone in his dining room picking at the watery fried eggs, undercooked hash browns, and almost burned beyond recognition toast that his cook had placed in front of him, was he worried? He worried so much he had trouble falling asleep at night, waking up in the morning feeling like someone had stuck bits of sandpaper to his eyeballs, with a dry throat, and the beginning of an ache somewhere between his chest and his stomach – he could never tell which.

Part of it, he knew, was the uncertainty of Dagastan's political situation. Dragov's people had moved quickly to take control of most of what passed for strategic points in the poor, landlocked country; the broadcast stations, the main military bases, and of course, the national bank. There'd been a total clamp down on information during the first three days. Embassy officials were hearing unsubstantiated rumors of certain 'enemies' of the new regime meeting untimely ends in basement cells or in remote villages to which foreigners were seldom welcome. Morgan had sought a meeting with Milosevic immediately after the coup, but hadn't learned anything that helped him predict in which direction the country would eventually go.

He did discover that winning Milosevic to the U.S. side, and somewhat away from the Soviet orbit in which the country had been since before World War II, had been the excuse Ellingsworth had used for his highly irregular clandestine meetings with the man. Whatever he'd achieved, unfortunately, had died with him. Milosevic wasn't opening up to Morgan or anyone else in the American embassy.

At first, Washington's silence was deafening. No one in the embassy could understand why they weren't being bombarded with queries from the various offices, bureaus, and agencies in the capital that all think themselves *primus inter pares* when it comes to where they stand in line to get their inane queries responded to. It didn't take Morgan long, however, to understand.

Just fifty-five days earlier, the last helicopter had lifted off from the embassy grounds in Saigon, ending the American presence in that country. Saigon's surrender to North Vietnamese forces that poured unopposed into the city had sent shock waves through official Washington. Even those members of Congress who had voted for cutting off funds for prosecuting the war were among those looking for someone to blame for its loss. That event alone, he knew, would have had the White House, the Pentagon, and the State Department pretty busy. But, it wasn't the only crisis or semi-crisis affecting a city that produced nothing really useful, just reams of laws, regulations and policies that people in the field had to try and make sense of. In mid-April, the Soviets had helped the Indians launch their first satellite, which had gotten the Pakistanis all spun up, and since Pakistan was Washington's main ally in that region, that was probably occupying dozens of analysts and desk officers. Domestically, the city was still reeling from the Watergate scandal. Several senior members of the Nixon administration had been convicted of a number of crimes, including a stupidly conducted break-in of the Democratic Party offices in the Watergate tower three years earlier. Nixon had himself resigned as president on August 9, 1974, putting his vice president, Gerald Ford in office to serve out the remainder of his two and a half year term. In its two hundred year history, with the Teapot Dome Scandal and all the other misbehavior the country had seen in its politicians, Tricky Dick became the first president in American history to resign from office.

No, Morgan knew; it would take something cataclysmic to refocus Washington's attention on a fourth-rate country in a third-rate part of the world; a country that didn't even have nuclear weapons.

He was still worrying, and kicking himself for it, during the ride from his residence, on a hill in a rather nice part of town – that is, if any part of a town dug out of the reddish brown loess of a plain that grew stunted corn and shaggy sheep could be called nice. At least, it didn't have the mud shanties occupied by rural peasants come to the city seeking their fortune only to find that, not only was there no fortune, but they were without the means to return to the countryside, that took up so much space in other parts of Kazbektun. His driver, who had taken a defensive driving course run by the State Department's Diplomatic Security Service, prided himself on varying his route every day, but always apologized profusely whenever the route took Morgan through areas of transients.

"Am sorry, boss," he would say. "Is too many peoples like this come to city now."

Every time he did it, Morgan would wave it off. He'd served in enough third world countries to no longer be affected by such sights.

Achmed pulled him up to his usual place, at the front entrance of the embassy, where he got out and went through the front door like all the other employees, and every visitor, through security and past Post One, where a Marine resplendent in his dress uniform saluted him and said a cheery, "Morning, sir." He always returned the salute. There was a special entrance in the back of the embassy that he could use, but he preferred letting people see him come to work.

He was just about to take the stairs to his office when he noticed Laura Pettigrew rush out to the front entry area, look around, shake her head, and return to the consular section, which was to the right of the main entrance foyer. She had a harried look on her face. His curiosity aroused, Morgan decided to pay a visit to the consular section before going to his office, where there would be nothing more interesting than the boring stack of overnight cables.

When he entered the section through the door reserved for employees, he saw Pettigrew, her round face red, and her feathery brown hair looking ruffled, talking to one of the four junior officers assigned to her section. Her normal doleful look was, today, one of frustration. As Morgan approached, she pointed toward the bank of windows where the other three vice consuls were busy interviewing visa applicants, and the harried looking young man rushed off to the nearest vacant window. She turned to Morgan.

"Morning, boss," she said. "To what do we owe the honor of your presence so early this fine morning?"

Morgan chuckled. Pettigrew's soulful brown eyes were always moist, as if she was about to cry at any instant; but, he knew that she was as tough as a Samurai's blade and as dangerous to tangle with as barbed wire. If she was harried, something was amiss.

"Just saw you rushing around like the proverbial headless chicken," he said. "So, I thought I'd drop in and see what's tough enough to flummox the unflummoxable Laura Pettigrew."

Her eyes went wide at the word 'unflummoxable,' which he'd just made up on the spot.

"Uh, yeah . . . well, if you look at the waiting room, you'll see what's flummoxing me. We have nearly twice our normal number of visa applicants today. Calvin, there was interviewing at his usual pace; about as fast as a beached whale; so I had to give him a little verbal stimulation to get him to move 'em through faster."

"What's causing such an upsurge in applications?"

She drew herself up to her full height, which was an inch short of Morgan's height, but the bulk of her body made her seem taller. An exasperated look creased her face.

"I've been kind of busy just trying to clear the waiting room and process them all," she said. "Of course, if you really must know, I'll have the officers ask. You know, one other thing that's strange; we have a lot more business people applying than usual too. I can't imagine what a business in the states is attracting so many Dagastani businessmen right now."

"That is strange," Morgan said. "Look, don't let it get in the way of getting the interviews done, but if you can let me know by the end of the day what's causing the rush, I'd appreciate it."

"Will do. Now, if you'll excuse me, I think I'd better pitch in and help with the interviews, or we'll be here until midnight."

Morgan recognized the tactful – bordering on blunt – dismissal. He smiled and turned on his heel, heading back to the stairwell and his office.

When he entered the executive suite, the first thing he saw was the empty desk where the ambassador's secretary normally sat. Vera Cotton, the Dragon Lady, who had been Ellingsworth's secretary, had packed and departed for the United States two days after his body was sent back under a ceremonial escort consisting of four of the marines from the security guard detachment and Montgomery Cornelius, the embassy's administrative officer. The door to the ambassador's office, which her desk effectively blocked, was closed. Morgan had had both her desk and the office thoroughly cleaned of personal effects, and checked by Pete Jeffers, the regional security officer (RSO) for any classified or sensitive material.

His secretary, the diminutive, but utterly efficient, Mary Sung, sat at her usual desk. Morgan had decided against moving to the ambassador's office. On the one hand, he didn't want the hassle of moving his gear, and on the other, when a new ambassador *was* selected, he didn't want the man or woman to arrive and having to move back to his office. Besides, he thought, he didn't need to get off on the wrong foot with the new boss.

Sung looked up as he approached, smiling slightly.

"Morning, Dave," she said. "You have visitors."

It was then that he noticed the three men sitting on the chairs just outside the door to his office. Dennis Larson, his acting DCM, recently-promoted Colonel Patrick Duggan, the Defense Attaché, and Pete Jeffers, the RSO, sat on the edge of the chairs, their faces a study in collective concern.

Shit, Morgan thought, *looks like my day is going to go from boringly bad to immeasurably worse.* "Okay, guys, let's go into my office."

Chapter Two

They hadn't even taken their seats before Duggan rounded on Morgan, his face reflecting more anxiety than both of the other men.

"Dave," he said. "I've been getting some disturbing news from my military contacts."

"Come on, Pat," Larson said. "We should give him some background before springing it on him like that."

Dennis Larson had a political officer's habit of prefacing every briefing with background information – 'to provide nuance,' he was fond of saying. Morgan personally preferred to get right to the point, and appreciated the army colonel's bluntness, but he had to give moral support to Larson, a man with a somewhat fragile ego, who always seemed to be intimidated by Duggan, and therefore, overcompensated by correcting him at every opportunity. Morgan spent a lot of time trying to figure out how to stop what he thought was counterproductive behavior – so far, to no avail.

"Dennis has a point, Pat," he finally said, coming down on the side of backing up his number two. Duggan was, as usual, unruffled.

"Yeah, I suppose so," he said. "My old contacts have finally decided it's okay to talk to me. In fact, since your meeting with Dragov, they've been downright garrulous. They've been telling me everything, a lot I really don't want to know. Lately, though, I've been picking up some signs of nervousness among the more senior officers. Last night, at a reception hosted by the British attaché, a Daggy colonel finally told me why."

Morgan didn't like the use of the term 'Daggy' to refer to their hosts, but the local employees in the embassy didn't seem offended, so he didn't make an issue of it. He never, though, used the term himself.

"Okay, I'll bite," he said. "Why are they nervous? Is Dragov doing another one of his purges?"

"No, nothing like that. He's pretty much cleaned the upper ranks of anyone whose loyalty was the least bit doubtful. Lots of new farmers out in the hinterlands. No, this has to do with their neighbors, the russkies. Seems they're frontier units are reporting a buildup of

Soviet forces near the western border crossing points."

"What kind of buildup?" Morgan asked.

"Well; his exact words were, Russian forces *massing* near the border. Now, you and I know that Ivan's always moving units around. Who knows why? Maybe they just like playing chess with military force. But, it seems a little far-fetched that they'd be planning a major move on a little back water like Dagastan. But, the guy was adamant; said he's sure they're planning to invade."

"Did he tell you what they're doing about it?"

That, for Morgan was a critical bit of information. If what Duggan was saying was true – hell, even if not true, the fact that a senior member of the local military was relating it to a foreigner – it would have to be reported to Washington, and the numb nut bureaucrats there, who had nothing better to do than ask endless, mind boggling questions, would immediately fire off cables asking for reams of supplementary information. By trying to answer as many of the questions in advance as possible, he knew he wouldn't prevent the cables, but at least he would know he'd given them the best possible information, and wouldn't feel too bad about ignoring the inevitable queries.

Duggan was shaking his head. That wasn't a

good sign.

"Well, Dave," the colonel said. "I tried to wheedle that little piece of info out of him, but he just kept shrugging and saying there was nothing to be done; whatever the fuck that means."

"It means the Dagastan military couldn't whip a gang of unruly girl scouts," a deep voice said from behind Morgan. He turned and saw that the station chief, Carlton Raine, had entered the office. He'd probably breezed past Mary Sung before she could react. "Sorry for busting in unannounced, but I was on the line to Langley, and just broke free."

Morgan could almost swear that there was a faint smile on Raine's brown face as he dropped his muscular frame into the empty chair at his left.

"You know anything about what's going on, Blood?" Morgan asked. Blood was Raine's nickname, but he would never tell anyone what it meant, leaving them to think it might be a reference to his race. Morgan suspected, though, that it was not.

"Not a whole hell of a lot more than Pat here," he said. "My contacts are being cagey, but when I talk to them, they're antsy, so I know something's up. They talk about worrying Soviet troop movements in the west, but I can't get anything beyond that – yet."

Morgan looked at Larson and Jeffers. "You two have anything to add to that?" he asked.

Larson looked at the young security officer.

"Tell him what you told me, Pete," he said.

"Well, boss," Jeffers said. "There's probably nothing to it, but some of my security guards are telling me that people in their neighborhoods are stockpiling food."

"To me," Larson said. "That's a pretty good indicator that something's brewing."

"Yeah, but what?" Morgan asked. "Hell, this place is on edge ninety percent of the time, and has been even antsier since the coup. Maybe there's an indication of a poor crop year; you think of that?"

Larson's cheeks reddened.

"Uh, well, not that hadn't occurred to me. I'll have Joe and his section check it out."

Joseph Wade was a bean pole of an economics officer who ran the embassy's economic reporting section. His 'section' consisted of himself, one junior officer, and a secretary he shared with Larson's section. To Morgan, he resembled a shaven version of Abraham Lincoln, and had the work habits of an absent minded Thomas Edison, but the man was a whiz at crunching numbers and making sense out of arcane events.

"Do that," he said. "Not, mind you, that I don't think your first hunch is right. It's beginning to fit together into an ugly picture; but, before we run to Washington with a cable claiming the sky's falling, I want a few pieces of sky to show them."

"You're right, of course," Larson said. "I guess I just got a little ahead of myself. So much has been happening lately, I didn't stop to think that there might be other factors that need consideration."

Morgan laid a hand softly on the younger man's arm.

"No harm, no foul, Dennis," he said gently. "We're all under a little pressure at the moment, myself included. There's no doubt we need to report this to Washington, and the sooner probably the better. But, we have to have our ducks in a row before we put anything in writing for the record – especially in light of recent events."

It had never been said, but Morgan knew in his gut that some in Washington were looking askance at him after Ellingsworth's death. Pete Jeffers worried about being an RSO who'd lost an ambassador, but many in the bureaucracy viewed the DCM as the individual in the embassy who had the responsibility for the care and feeding of the ambassador. During all his time in the service, Morgan hadn't heard of an ambassador being killed under similar circumstances. All that meant, though, was that the bureaucrats didn't have a precedent. *Damn,* he thought, *what a way to get your name in the history books. Getting your ambassador assassinated in a country that American wasn't at war with.* He had little doubt that what lay in store for him would be anything but pleasant.

"Here's what we do," he said, shaking himself out of the reverie that threatened to become a blue funk. "Pat, throw lines out to all your contacts, at all levels. See what they have to say. Blood; I know your sources are close hold, but see if you can get anything from any of them. Pete, get your guards to snoop around their communities and see if they can get any details about what's going on. Get all your reports to Dennis who'll coordinate a summary and do the first draft of our cable to Washington."

Everyone nodded. Larson and Duggan took notes.

"Let's meet back here at sixteen hundred hours," Morgan continued. He noticed a puzzled look on Larson's face. "That's four pm, Dennis. Sorry, I guess I lapsed back into a military mode of thinking and speaking. Anyway, we'll meet then and see where we are on this."

For Morgan, the rest of the day moved like a fat man in the supermarket checkout line who has to stop and read all the tabloid headlines, just when the ice cream you bought has started to melt. He wasn't a micromanager by nature, having learned in the army that the sure way to kill initiative and piss your subordinates off is to look over their shoulders while they're trying to get done what you've told them to get done. In this case, though, he had to restrain himself from popping into Dennis Larson's office to see what he'd learned. He forced himself to focus his mind on the other paperwork that seemed to copulate and reproduce in his inbox every night; initialing reports of vehicle usage, making marginal notes on a dense report on sorghum crop yields prepared by one of the youngsters in the economics section, and annotating one of the consular section's reports with a 'well done' in his characteristic script.

With the routine stuff out of the way, he turned his attention to the items he felt he not only had to read, but understand. Things like Pete Jeffers' report of criminal activity, or information reports from the defense attaché or the station – information reports, because they didn't become intelligence until the analysts in Washington vetted and checked them. Some of the reports were days old – having gone through other hands for 'concurrence' before reaching his desk. None of them contained anything of real interest. The report that would be interesting reading hadn't been written yet, because they didn't know enough.

He ate his lunch at his desk; not because he had so much work to do, but because if he ate in the embassy cafeteria, he'd have to make small talk with members of the staff, and he didn't feel like small talk. Mary Sung was kind enough to fetch him a ham sandwich and a coke from the cafeteria, which he wolfed down without even tasting.

When four came, he was waiting at his office door. Carlton Raine, followed closely by Dennis Larson, came into the executive area precisely at four. A couple of minutes later, Duggan and Jeffers arrived. Morgan ushered them into his office.

Just as they were settling themselves around the low table in the corner, Sung came in, a frown on her round, brown face.

"Dave, Laura Pettigrew is here to see you," she said. "I told her you were in an important meeting, but she insists that what she has is more important."

"A damn sight more important than a meeting of the good old boys," the hefty consular chief said as she pushed past Sung and walked into Morgan's office.

Chapter Three

Pettigrew walked over and, with her hands on her ample hips, stared down at the five men. They looked up at her with the expressions of boys caught with their hands in the cookie jar.

"It's not what you think it is, Laura," Morgan said. There was a shade too much defensiveness in his voice. He cleared his throat. "We're just about to discuss what's going on in this country right now in order to prepare our report to Washington."

"Well, in that case, what I have to say will be of interest."

"What could possibly be of interest from the consular section?" Larson asked.

Morgan wanted to reach over and slap the younger man. So like political officers, he thought, thinking that they were the only ones who ever did anything important. He recalled his conversation with Pettigrew earlier in the day. She could just have the information they needed to add credibility to a report.

"Did you get the information I asked for this morning?" he asked mildly.

He tried to keep any note of censure out of his voice, but Pettigrew picked up on his meaning nonetheless, and couldn't resist twisting the barb.

"Yes, I did," she said with a note of smug satisfaction. "If you want to know what's really happening in a country, you don't go sucking up to the foreign minister, or even your military buddies." Her look of mild scorn took in everyone except Pete Jeffers. Morgan suspected that she was a bit sweet on the young security man. "No, what you do is ask a consular officer to get it out of the people who'll do or say anything to get their hands on an American visa."

Morgan could only let her go on so long. He still had to maintain order and control.

"And, what did you learn?" he asked.

"I can sum it up in four words, the Russians are coming," she said. "I had my guys start asking applicants why they wanted to leave the country, and almost every one of them said it's because they think the Russians are about to invade."

"That's all well and good," Larson said. "But, what evidence do they offer to support their belief?"

The man, Morgan thought, was clearly upset at Pettigrew upstaging what he viewed as a 'substantive' meeting with her 'consular' matters, but he did have a point; they couldn't go to Washington with nothing more than 'increasing numbers of visa applicants are saying they want to leave the country because the Russians are about to invade.'

"Did any of them give any concrete reasons for believing an invasion is imminent?" he asked Pettigrew, who seemed totally unaffected by Larson's skepticism.

"Not at first," she said. "But, I interviewed a few myself; mostly the business people. A couple of them came from the country's western region, and they both said that not only have they seen a lot of Russian tanks near the border, but one said he's sure he saw Russian soldiers skulking in the hills near his village."

"Advance scouting parties, no doubt," Duggan said. "Shit, Dave, sounds like an invasion to me."

"So," Larson said. "A few Soviets cross the border, so what? That doesn't make an invasion."

Duggan looked at him down his long nose.

"Son, I don't expect you to understand military strategy," he said, his voice dripping with condescension. "But, reconnaissance missions will almost always precede main forces crossing the FEBA – that's forward edge of the battle area, by the way. The only logical thing that explains scouts on this side of the border and tanks that close to the border on the other side is the damn russkies plan to invade."

"I agree," Morgan said, more to forestall any further bickering than anything else, because he could see Larson's cheeks darken, and his mouth begin to open. "Okay, Dennis, I think we have enough at least for a preliminary cable. Everyone get what you have to Dennis right away." He pointedly included Pettigrew in that instruction. "I want something on my desk in an hour."

He smiled as everyone filed out of his office. They just needed some firm direction, he thought. *Damn, I haven't lost it, even after all these years.* 'It' was his ability to command men – well, actually, people was a better word. During his time in the army, he'd only every encountered women rarely, and then mainly as nurses or adjutant general types, which is basically another way of saying overpaid clerks. He'd spent his entire career in combat units, mostly Special Forces; organizations that hadn't opened their ranks to women. Since joining the

Foreign Service, he'd met a few more women in leadership roles; his former ambassador being a case in point; but only a few.

He also knew that Larson, for all his somewhat officious behavior, would have a cable polished and ready to go at the requested time. His ability to take a collection of apparently disparate facts and weave them into a coherent dispatch was phenomenal. If only he had better people skills, Morgan thought, he'd make a fine leader someday.

Chapter Four

Larson hadn't disappointed. The draft dispatch he placed on Morgan's desk fifty-six minutes after leaving his office, needed very little editing. Morgan gave it a careful read, and then initialed in the upper right hand corner approving its transmission to Washington.

FROM: AMEMBASSY KAZEBKTUN

TO: SECSTATE WASHDC
INFO: SECDEF WASHDC//J2//
WHITE HOUSE WASHDC

SECRET NOFORN

NIACT IMMEDIATE

STATE FOR DAGASTAN COUNTRY DIRECTOR
WHITE HOUSE FOR NSC

SUBJECT: INDICATIONS OF SOVIET MOVE ON
DAGASTAN

1. SUMMARY: EMBOFFS HAVE RECEIVED
    INCREASING INDICATIONS OF A POSSIBLE
    MOVE OF SOVIET FORCES INTO DAGASTAN
    ACROSS THE WESTERN BORDER. WE
    BELIEVE THIS TO BE IN RESPONSE TO
    RECENT COUP AND NEW GOVERNMENT'S
    OVERTURES TO USG. WILL REPORT AS
    SITUATION DEVELOPS.

2. OFFICERS OF THIS EMBASSY HAVE
    RECEIVED A NUMBER OF COMMUNICATIONS
    FROM CONTACTS WITHIN DAGASTANI
    GOVERNMENT AND SOCIETY, INDICATING A
    BUILDUP OF SOVIET MILITARY FORCES NEAR
    BORDER CROSSING POINTS ON THE
    WESTERN BORDER. THERE HAVE ALSO BEEN
    REPORTS OF POSSIBLE SOVIET SCOUTING
    UNITS INSIDE DAGASTAN ITSELF. WE
    BELIEVE THIS IS AN INDICATION OF A
    POSSIBLE MOVE OF SOVIET FORCES TO
    ENSURE THAT DAGASTAN REMAINS WITHIN
    ITS SPHERE OF INFLUENCE.

3. EMBASSY DATT REPORTS THAT MILITARY
    CONTACTS HAVE REPORTED INCREASED
    NUMBERS OF TANK AND INFANTRY FORCES
    IN PROXIMITY TO BORDER POINTS IN THE
    WEST. THEY BELIEVE THIS BUILDUP IS A
    SIGN THAT THEIR RUSSIAN NEIGHBORS PLAN
    TO INVADE. DATT REPORTS INCREASED
    NERVOUSNESS AMONG MANY SENIOR AND
    MIDLEVEL MILITARY OFFICERS.

4. POLOFF'S SOURCES SAY THAT THE
    INSTABILITY THAT IMMEDIATELY FOLLOWED
    THE RECENT COUP IN WHICH FORMER

DEPUTY COMMANDER OF STATE SECURITY,
OUSTED FORMER FIRST SECRETARY DMITRI
KOVASC HAS CEASED. THERE WERE A FEW
ARRESTS AND (QUOTE) DISAPPEARANCES
(END QUOTE), BUT SUCH EVENTS WERE
MINIMAL.

5. CONOFF REPORTS SIGNIFICANT INCREASE IN
VISA APPLICATIONS, WITH APPLICANTS
STATING THAT FEAR OF RUSSIAN INVASION
IS ONE OF THE MAIN REASONS THEY WANT
TO LEAVE. A NUMBER OF APPLICANTS ALSO
REPORT SEEING LARGE NUMBERS OF
RUSSIAN FORCES NEAR BORDER, AND WHAT
THEY BELIEVED TO BE RUSSIAN SOLDIERS
INSIDE DAGASTAN ITSELF, IN THE HILLS TO
THE WEST OF THE CAPITAL.

6. COMMENT: AT THIS POINT, WE CAN'T STATE
CATEGORICALLY THAT A SOVIET INCURSION
INTO DAGASTAN IS IMMINENT, BUT BELIEVE
IT MOST LIKELY. POST IS WORKING TO
OBTAIN MORE PRECISE DETAILS AND WILL
REPORT THEM AS WE GET THEM. MOOD IN
THE CAPITAL, OTHER THAN ABOVE-
MENTIONED NERVOUSNESS OF OUR
CONTACTS, IS CALM. WE DON'T BELIEVE
THERE IS ANY SIGNIFICANT THREAT TO
EMBASSY OR ITS PERSONNEL, BUT ARE
PUTTING INCREASED SECURITY MEASURES
IN PLACE TO BE PRUDENT.

MORGAN

He ensured that the document was
appropriately classified, wondering if maybe
SECRET was a bit too high, and then deciding
that any lower classification would probably

result in it being ignored, and gave it to Mary Sung to be delivered immediately to the communications section which had remained open and on standby waiting for it. He knew that the NIACT IMMEDIATE, signifying that this was an urgent communication requiring night action if necessary, would get attention. Dagastan might be a backwater, but Washington's bureaucracy was genetically predisposed to action when the appropriate tags were put on paperwork.

Now, it was a matter of keeping one ear to the local ground, in order to maintain situational awareness, and the other cocked in the direction of Washington, to be able to respond to whatever cockamamie ideas they came up with.

Morgan was whistling as he turned out his office light and headed downstairs for the ride home.

Chapter Five

Washington reacted faster than he'd anticipated.

As he entered his residence, he could hear the warbling of the secure phone he'd had installed in the little room off the living room that he used as a home office. He'd often suggested that Ellingsworth put one in, but the man had resisted. After assuming temporary charge, he'd gotten Jeffers to agree and had instructed the communications officer to put one in his residence. It meant he no longer had to get up in the middle of the night and make the long trip across town over streets that were more pothole than surface, just to return a sensitive call. Of course, like now, it meant he could no longer get away from the idle minds in the bureaucracy who seemed to be unaware of the ten-hour time difference.

He tossed his briefcase on the table near the entrance where his butler normally put the guest book on those rare occasions when he entertained, and went into the office.

"Morgan here," he said when he picked up the phone. "How can I help you?"

It sounded trite; even dumb; but, he almost always answered the phone in that manner.

"Mr. Morgan," a wavery voice said. "I'm Samuel Gosnell, the new desk officer for Dagastan. Just got through reading your cable. Hot stuff. I have to prepare a brief for the assistant secretary, and I have a few questions."

And, now it starts. Everything we know is in the fucking cable. There hasn't been enough time for things to change. Morgan said none of this. He didn't blame the poor desk officer, who was probably just following instructions from a country director, who had been told by a deputy assistant secretary to make sure of the details before preparing the briefing for the assistant secretary. In addition, the deputy assistant secretary had probably been called by some political appointee sitting behind a desk somewhere on the seventh floor of the cavernous State Department building, and told to make sure the briefing reflected well on the administration. This was just idle speculation on his part of course. Morgan had avoided an assignment to Foggy Bottom like a cat avoids water.

"Okay," he said. "But, before you start with the questions, I have to tell you that I don't know anything more than what was in the cable we just sent less than an hour ago."

There was a long pause, the only sound the warbling whistle of the secure phone connection. Then, Gosnell's distorted voice came over the headset, "I sort of figured that, but I was told to call and check just in case. So, there've been no further developments?"

"That's right. If you'll give me your number, I'll be sure to call you as soon as anything happens."

Gosnell gave Morgan the number to the secure phone in the country directorate, as well as his home number. "If it's after hours here you can call me directly," he said. "We'll just have to be careful to keep the conversation sanitized."

Yeah, Morgan thought as he broke the connection, as if someone's listening or even gives a shit about what goes on out here in the back and beyond. He was looking forward to a light supper, some light reading to put him in the proper frame of mind, and a good night's sleep, the first since, as Duggan so aptly said, 'the shit hit the fan.'

Chapter Six

Tuesday, June 24, 1975, Washington, DC

At 7:31 am, the loud bell in the State Department's main communication center rang, signaling that a NIACT-Immediate cable was coming over the wire. The duty communicator put his coffee mug down on top of the *Playboy* magazine he'd been reading, placing it directly on the well-developed mammaries of the Playmate of the Month, and walked over to the large bank of machines that sat whirring and chiming along one wall.

As the long mauve tape spit out of the slot, he took it and inserted it into the machine that would translate the perforations in the tape into typed words, numbers and symbols on the paper in the tray at the bottom. Quickly, sheets started dropping into a basket at the side, all nicely collated and stapled. He could see that the message was short, and only five copies came out; one for his files, one for the main addressee in the State Department, one for the Executive Secretariat, which received a copy of every incoming cable except for a few which were for restricted or EYES ONLY distribution, and one for the Bureau of Intelligence and Research (INR), which also got a copy of anything that might contain intelligence information. He picked up the fifth copy and saw that it was for the White House. Cables from embassies addressed for anyone at 1600 Pennsylvania Avenue were actually printed out at the State Department on C Street and delivered by courier.

The man wasted no time. He called two couriers. One to deliver the three copies to those within the building, and another to take the other copy to the White House. The cables were put in folders with red-bordered cardboards attached signifying their SECRET classification, and would not leave the couriers' hands until signed for by the intended recipients. The fifth copy went into the incoming message folder on his desk, which would be filed away at the end of the day.

The internal courier went first to the country directorate, knowing that this is where any response or reaction to the message would eventually come. Had no one been available to sign for it, he would have gone to the nearest phone and notified his supervisor, who would have contacted the Operations Center, which is manned around the clock, to have them call someone in. That's the drill with any document marked NIACT. As luck would have it, Samuel Gosnell, the newly assigned desk officer for Dagastan, was in, had, in fact, been at his desk since six that morning.

A lanky Midwesterner with hair that couldn't decide whether it was brown or blond, he was on his third Foreign Service tour, having done two tours abroad, one in Nairobi, Kenya as a visa officer, and a second in the embassy in Warsaw, Poland as a junior political officer. A grade three officer, he was looking to his current job to get him promoted to grade two, and hoping that, if he did it well, he might even be considered for a deputy chief of mission job at one of the small embassies, or at a minimum, political section chief somewhere.

So, naturally, he came in early, stayed late, and forever tried to know what his bosses wanted before they did.

The cable, therefore, caught him by surprise. He'd been on the job for three weeks, and during that time, nothing had happened. He wasn't sure he was ready for this – a military invasion the first month of the job. Damn, he thought, what do I do now?

After a bit of reflection, he realized that the smart thing to do was consult his superior. Gaylord Pepper, head of the country directorate, hadn't been on the job much longer than Gosnell. But, he was senior, and had, Gosnell thought, probably experienced something akin to this at some point during his career.

He was surprised, then, when Pepper immediately grabbed his arm and nearly dragged him to the office of Montgomery Jackson-Leigh, the deputy assistant secretary of defense responsible for the region. And, that worthy just instructed Gosnell to go back and call the embassy for further information.

He'd run, or been run, around in a big circle. He felt a bit odd calling to ask for more information just hours after the message had been written, and knowing the time difference, when the authors would be heading home after a long and, based on the content of the cable, grueling day. But, there was nothing for it.

Gosnell's conversation with David Morgan, charge d'affaires of the embassy, had been brief, but not unpleasant. Morgan impressed him as the type who would never have given such a bureaucratically inane and ultimately useless instruction.

He made a note of Morgan's phone number and the content of their conversation, typed up an Info Memo, or summary of what he'd done since receiving the initial cable, attached it to a copy of the cable with a paper clip, and gave it to Pepper's secretary. An elderly woman with slightly purple hair, she'd worked as secretary for a succession of officials throughout the State Department, had seen it all, and been impressed by very little of it. She thanked Gosnell, tossed the package in a tray on the edge of her desk, and returned to whatever it was she'd been typing, blotting him from her mind.

In another part of the building, in the windowless spaces inhabited by the analysts of INR, Alison Chambers, a senior analyst, had also come to work early. When the courier dropped the cable off with the secretary who sat in the reception area and provided support to several analysts, she took one look at it and walked to Chambers' door.

"Hey, girl," the tall black woman said. "I got something here I think you'll be interested in."

Chambers had been hunched over her desk, trying to find a location on a faded and wrinkled old map. She looked up at the secretary, envying her ability to keep her iron gray hair immaculately groomed, and to be able to smile, even before the start of the official work day, in what amounted to a metal-enclosed cage.

"Morning, Earline," she said. "What could be more important than driving myself blind trying to find a place that probably doesn't exist on a map that's all wrong anyway?"

The secretary handed her the message and stepped back, a half smile on her smooth, brown face. When Chambers had finished reading, she looked up, her eyes wide with concern.

"Okay, you were right. This just come in?"

"Honey, you been in this job long enough to know how to read a date-time-group. Look at that one. That was sent less than an hour ago. They must've had to stay after hours to do it."

Chambers, who had taken to wearing her brown hair cut short, in an almost page boy style, ran her hand through it as she looked at the string of numbers and letters at the top of the message. The secretary was right; this *was* hot off the press.

She'd almost put Dagastan out of her mind. Almost getting killed, and watching a man get gunned down right in front of her eyes, had traumatized her for weeks. But for Lee Kennedy, not only would she be dead, she'd probably be institutionalized for mental instability. Thinking of the diplomatic security agent who had saved her life – and more – she felt a warm sensation all over her body, and a smile crept onto her face. *Whoa, girl. Get your mind out of the gutter and back to business. Things are going south in a hurry in Dagastan, and you'll need all your wits to deal with it no doubt.*

"Yeah, I see it," she said. "Thanks for bringing this to me. I owe you one."

"Girl, you owe me more than one. I didn't pass that to you, you know one of the male analysts likely to grab it."

"How about I buy you lunch today?"

"Deal, but not downstairs. I want to go somewhere nice, like one of them fancy restaurants up near the university."

Chambers winced. That would be expensive. But, the woman deserved it. She looked out for her; one woman taking care of another.

"Okay, let's plan to leave a bit before noon so we can maybe catch a table on the sidewalk. I know just the place."

When the woman had gone, Chambers read the cable again. It didn't say much, but then, initial reports seldom did. She fought down the impulse to pick up the phone and call the embassy for more information. She'd never met David Morgan, but had spoken to him on the phone, and seen the results of his work. She trusted that he'd keep everyone suitably informed.

It was troubling, though. With everything that was going on, another trouble spot in the world would complicate everyone's life. And, after almost getting killed because of a country she'd never visited, and hadn't been able to find easily on a map when she first heard of it, having it come up again in the context of a crisis wasn't how she wanted to spend her time. But, she had the file. That made it her case.

She picked up the phone and dialed the number of the Dagastan desk. She'd only met the previous desk officer, Lesley Carter, on a couple of occasions. She'd been killed before Chambers got a chance to get to know her. It was her death, in fact, that drew Chambers into the murky situation that revolved around Dagastan. At the thought, she felt a pang of sadness. At the same time, there was happiness involved. It was thanks to the mess that had started with Carter's death that had thrown her and Lee Kennedy together. And, that relationship was progressing nicely, thank you very much. She had yet to meet the new desk officer; couldn't remember his name; so, she was grateful when he answered with, "Dagastan desk, Samuel Gosnell speaking. How may I help you?"

She identified herself and mentioned the cable. Gosnell told her that he'd just gotten off the phone with David Morgan, and there was nothing further to report at the moment. She breathed a sigh of relief that it hadn't been her to call poor Morgan so late. Thanking Gosnell for his information, she pressed the button to terminate the call.

Without putting the phone down, she dialed

Lee's extension.

"Kennedy here," his deep voice came over the line. Even over the phone, his voice gave her shivers.

"Lee, it's Alison," she said. "What are you doing for lunch today?"

"Nothing in particular; what did you have in mind?"

She told him her plans to take the secretary Earline to lunch, and asked if he'd like to tag along.

"You're not planning to eat in the cafeteria are you?" he asked.

"Of course not. I thought we'd go up around GWU and try one of those sidewalk restaurants."

"Well then, count me in. Meet you in the E Street lobby?"

She could hear his throaty chuckle as she put the phone down.

Chapter Seven

Lee Kennedy was waiting just outside the big glass doors to the E Street lobby, which is the main employee entrance to the Department of State, when the two women came out of the elevator. He smiled broadly when he saw Alison striding across the tiles toward him. Even in a plain business dress, she was the most beautiful woman he'd seen in a long time.

He had to restrain himself from pulling her into his arms and kissing her when she walked up to him. The tall black woman, he had to search his memory for her name – Earline – smiled knowingly at him.

"Well, if it isn't the knight in shining armor," she said. "Haven't seen you around in a while."

She nudged Chambers arm. "I was afraid you two might have broken up or something."

Kennedy and Chambers both blushed.

"Earline, really!" Chambers said.

"What's the matter? You two think I didn't notice the way you were making eyes at each other? Shoot, girl, everybody in the building knows you two were an item."

"Guess there's no point in trying to keep it a secret," Kennedy said.

Chambers blushed some more.

"Well, at least you haven't broken up," the secretary said. "Now, let's go get some food; I'm starved."

As the three of them, laughing and chatting, left the vicinity of the big building that sits sandwiched between C and E Street, with the Department of Interior to its east and a navy medical installation on its west, in a corner office on the third floor, near where corridor 8 and corridor 5 cross, where the Bureau of Personnel has its offices, a thin faced woman with a long thin nose that nearly touched her top lip, her dirty yellow hair pulled back severely and tied in a bun, and dressed in a one-piece black dress that draped loosely on her gaunt frame, sat on an uncomfortable chair against the wall, just inside the door to the office that handled secretarial assignments.

Vera Cotton had been coming to the same office, sitting in the same chair, for a week now. A week of fruitless, futile waiting for a new assignment as a secretary, preferably for an ambassador somewhere, but an assistant secretary would do. But, each day she got the same answer; 'sorry, none of those jobs are open at the moment, but we have a position in the Foreign Buildings Office you might be interested in.' Yeah, she thought, each time it came up, trying to exile me to FBO; out of sight, out of mind.

She knew that she was damaged goods. Her ambassador had been killed, and while the events leading up to Robert Ellingsworth's death had been completely beyond her control, she knew that the *system* considered her bad luck at the moment. Bad news in this organization spreads faster than a gasoline-stoked brush fire, she thought, or as fast as a cold virus among a class of kindergarten students. She was surprised they hadn't suggested she take some course at the Foreign Service Institute. She could be hidden in FSI's Rosslyn building for months, and the personnel system wouldn't have to deal with her.

It wasn't fair, she thought. She'd done nothing wrong. She'd served the ambassador faithfully. Why should she be the one having to suffer?

It was that bastard, David Morgan, she

thought. He was the one always nitpicking at everything poor Robert Ellingsworth did. He and Pete Jeffers had been with him when he was shot. She'd never been told what that meeting was all about – didn't even know it had been scheduled in fact. A thought had been forming in the recesses of her mind, those dark areas where evil thoughts tend to germinate. Now, sitting here, fuming over her inability to get an assignment befitting her experience; that thought began to move from the dark back room of her mind toward the well-lit front room and the light of day.

Suddenly, she stood. So suddenly, she startled the young redhead manning the reception desk. She knew what she had to do.

Without a word, and ignoring the gape-mouthed stare of the secretary, she yanked open the door and spun out into the corridor. Getting her bearings, she turned on her heels and headed for the office of the director general of the Foreign Service.

Chapter Eight

Tuesday, June 24, 1975, Puntarenas, *Costa Rica*

Sitting on the verandah of a little cottage nestled in the palm trees on a little rise overlooking the white sandy beaches and the Pacific Ocean beyond, Niles Hitchcock was bored.

For weeks now, he'd done little else but sit on the verandah, listening to the raucous sound of the birds in the lush foliage – almost a jungle – at the rear of the cottage, and the incessant roar of the ocean as it pounded the beach. After the Committee had exiled him for his role in the events in Dagastan and Washington, he'd considered staying in Costa Rica's capital city, San Jose. But, he decided that if he was to stay out of sight, a small beach town like

Puntarenas, where there were a lot of American tourists and a few expats who, like him, stayed to themselves, so he didn't draw much attention.

The problem with that was that Niles Hitchcock *liked* getting attention.

Had it not been for the stupid overreaching of Carlton Longroux, the late senator from the state of Alabama, he'd still be in Washington where things were happening, and where he got the attention he knew he deserved. Longroux just couldn't keep his mouth shut, and was always going a step farther than other, more prudent souls thought wise. It had been him who'd hired that knife-wielding thug who'd left a trail of bodies in DC, a trail that had led the committee right to Hitchcock's doorstep, and to his expulsion from the Committee.

And, that's how he viewed it – an expulsion. Oh sure, Jonathan Appleby, the current chairman of the Committee, had told him that it was just temporary until the heat was off. But, Hitchcock didn't trust the senator from North Dakota; his folksy speech and cornball cowboy attire were just props to put his victims at ease. Underneath that Will Rogers exterior, Hitchcock knew, was a con man who'd steal the dirt from beneath your fingernails. Appleby probably viewed Hitchcock as a rival for leadership of the group, and had used Longroux's mistakes; which, truth be told, were as much his fault as the late senator's, but since there was no one around to contradict him, Hitchcock didn't even admit to himself that he was in any way responsible; as an excuse. That's all it was. A naked power grab. But, it had worked. Appleby was comfortably in Washington, pulling strings as usual, while he, Niles Hitchcock, sat in a wicker chair on a porch whose floor boards creaked annoyingly, looking at the same patch of blue sky he'd been eyeing all morning.

"No way, dammit," he said to the sky. "Niles Hitchcock doesn't roll over and play dead for anyone."

He glared down at the glass of rum in his hand. The dark brown, fiery liquor had been his only solace, but of late he knew he'd been going to that well far too often. He rubbed at his chin, making a raspy sound. Dammit, he'd forgotten to shave again. Niles Hitchcock was fussy about his appearance. He never went out in public without shaving, or being attired appropriately in coat and tie. Yet, for weeks now, he'd gone days sometimes without shaving, and as he looked down, he saw that he was barefoot and wearing a pair of torn khakis and a dirty T-shirt.

He growled and threw the glass out over the railing of the verandah. It made a swooshing sound as it dropped into the flowery shrubs that lined the white stone walk up from the beach.

"Goddammit, enough is enough. I can't live another day like this. Appleby and those other pricks be damned. I'm going back where I belong."

Chapter Nine

Wednesday, June 25, 1975, Washington, DC

The two men sat in one of the smaller conference rooms down the hall from the director general's office. One, young, sandy haired, wearing a three-piece gray suit even in the beginning of what promised to be a sultry summer, was the DG's special assistant. The other, several years older, wearing a somewhat rumpled brown suit, his green tie's knot askew, and a middle-age paunch pushing against the buttons of his jacket, was principal assistant to the director of personnel. They had been assigned to deal with a problem that had presented itself to the director general the previous day.

"The DG wants this problem to go away," the young special assistant said.

"Can you be sure this woman's claims are

even valid?" the older man responded wearily.

"It hardly matters, does it? If she tells her story to someone else, oh say, someone in the political leadership of this place, it'll start all kinds of messes. The director general doesn't want to involve the politicians if she can avoid it."

"Yeah, but I had my people research this Cotton woman. She has a reputation; do you know what her nickname is among Foreign Service Officers?"

"I heard she's called Dragon Lady," the young man said. "So, she's a tough old bird. That doesn't make her accusations invalid."

"But, she's accusing a senior officer of a pretty serious offense. Did she offer any proof? No? I didn't think so. And, then there's the issue of the officer she's accusing. The DG of all people should be sensitive to the implications of that."

"This Morgan fellow; I don't know him. What's his story?"

"He's a veteran, got combat service in Vietnam in the early days of the war. He came into the Foreign Service through the examination process ten years ago. So far, he's had a good record. Thing is, he's a minority. Going after a black officer on something like this, if there's no evidence to support it, is not going to look good. We've been taking enough of a beating for the Foreign Service being overwhelmingly male, pale and Yale as it is."

The young man sighed and shrugged.

"I appreciate the dilemma. But, consider it from another angle – just as fraught with difficulties – a woman, who happens to be a secretary, has made an accusation against a senior generalist officer. If we do nothing, it'll look like we're insensitive to both women employees and support staff."

"Shit," the older man said. "We're damned if we do, and damned if we don't. I really need to retire. This job's starting to get to me."

"Look, I sympathize with you, but I have to tell the DG something. What do you plan to do?"

"We'd really like to *do* nothing; but, I realize that's not an option. The challenge is to be seen as doing something without irreparably damaging a possibly innocent person's career." The older man fiddled with a folder of papers on the table in front of him. "We've decided to ask the bureau to recall him for consultations. Once he's back here, we'll do a rump accountability review board to try and get at the facts."

The young man nodded and made a note on the pad in front of him.

"That should keep everyone happy." Pause.

"At least for a while." A longer pause. "Just between you and me, though; do you think there's anything to these allegations?"

It was now the older man's turn to pause. He regarded his young colleague over the top of horn-rim spectacles resting on the end of his nose.

Finally, he spoke, "Something went horribly wrong in Dagastan. We might never know what, but there's more to this situation than meets the eye. I don't know David Morgan personally, but he has a good corridor reputation. A solid performer and, with his military background, someone people say you can count on in a difficult situation. This woman Cotton seems to be accusing him of deliberately getting Robert Ellingsworth killed. That I don't believe. As to the rest; we'll just have to wait and see how it works out."

"Whatever you do, just keep it off the seventh floor, and for Christ's sake, try and keep it out of the press."

"Good luck with both of those quixotic quests. It's just a matter of time until our real reason for calling him back here gets out within the building. Once that happens, it's out of our hands. Once we start probing the incident, we have to let him know he's entitled to have legal counsel or assistance from the union."

"Oh shit, if AFSA gets involved, all bets are

off," the young man said.

"The American Foreign Service Association *is* the bargaining unit for all Foreign Service employees," the man from personnel said. "Legally, we are bound to ensure he has access to them."

The young man shook his head.

"Heaven help us," he said.

Chapter Ten

As the officials from the director general's office and the office of personnel were concluding their meeting, David Morgan's fate was being discussed in another part of the building.

Alison Chambers, concerned that she'd heard nothing further on what was happening in Dagastan, called Samuel Gosnell, the Dagastan desk officer.

"Mr. Gosnell, have you heard anything from the embassy about what's going on out there?" she asked breathlessly when he answered.

"No, Ms. Chambers, and would you please call me Sam or Samuel? It makes me nervous when people call me mister."

"Okay, Sam it is. I'm Alison. Isn't it a bit strange not hearing anything?"

"I don't think so; it's only been a day. There've been no press reports, so there's a good chance this is just a false alarm."

Chambers knew he could be right, but she had a feeling in the center of her gut he wasn't. Something was going on, and her gut was telling her it wasn't good.

"What's the mood among your higher ups?"

She was trolling, and she knew it, but often the back room conversations were a good indication of what the ultimate policy position would be. At a minimum, she felt maybe a little gossip would help her decide what avenues of inquiry she should pursue.

There was a long pause at the other end of the line. Mentally, Chambers could see the desk officer wondering how much to trust her. "I just want some idea of what direction you policy wonks are going, so I can shape my information requests to support it," she added, hoping it would allay any suspicions he might have.

"Well . . . look, what I'm about to tell you is extremely sensitive, and I'd appreciate it if you never let anyone know you heard it from me," Gosnell finally said.

"Hey, Sam, I'm an intelligence analyst. I know how to keep secrets."

"My boss had a meeting with the DAS early this morning," he said. "He didn't tell me everything that was discussed, but I got the feeling they've decided to throw poor Dave Morgan to the wolves."

"Huh? What does that mean?" Chambers asked.

"Well, I'm not completely sure. The late ambassador's secretary is supposedly saying that Morgan was responsible for Ambassador Ellingsworth's death. Scuttlebutt is that at some point today personnel will contact us and ask that we call him back to Washington for, uh, consultations."

"It's a bit foolish to pull the guy in charge out in the middle of a crisis, but chiefs of mission get called back for consultations all the time."

"Yeah, only there won't be any consultations. Personnel plans to grill him about what happened to the ambassador. They're even saying he might need a lawyer."

Chambers felt as if someone had just slapped her. *I'll bet the same people who started all this are behind it,* she thought. *Just like them to try and shift the blame to the one innocent person in the whole mess.* "Wow," was what she said to Gosnell. "That's pretty heavy. Look, without getting yourself in trouble, could you keep me posted on what's going on?"

"I'll do my best. No promises, though. I've

got too much invested in my career to risk pissing off the wrong people."

Nice thing about being Civil Service rather than Foreign Service, Chambers thought; it's a lot harder to fire you. Oh, they can get back at you in a thousand little ways – shit assignments, not inviting you to meetings, etc. – but, poor Gosnell could have his career chopped in the neck if he stepped too far wrong, or was just on the wrong side of an issue. Look at poor David Morgan.

"Shit," she said after she'd broken the connection. "Will this never end?"

Chapter Eleven

Thursday, June 26, 1975, Dagastan

Morgan found himself whistling softly as he took the stairs two at a time going from the lobby to his office. It's funny, he thought; when things are peaceful, I fret. But, when everything's topsy turvy and the roof's about to cave in, I get cheerful. It had been the same way during his two tours in Vietnam. When he was stuck at a fire base with nothing to do but drink tepid Lone Star beer and watch 8 millimeter movies at the officers' club tent, he was antsy and out of sorts. As soon as he left a chopper on a hot LZ with Charlie throwing shit at them from all sides, he calmed down and felt alive.

No one in Dagastan was trying to blow him away with an AK or an RPG – yet, but the rumors of Soviet tanks and infantry units at the border kept coming in. With so much smoke, there had to be a flicker of a flame somewhere.

He was in his element. Decisions to make. Actions to check. Even though he'd been a Signal Corps officer in the army, Morgan had volunteered for infantry duty when he was sent to Vietnam. The first time, it was hard to convince the weenies in S-1 that a captain with crossed signal flags could handle an infantry unit, but he'd been a natural. His men learned to respect him, and after a few weeks in command, his guys would follow him into hell, which was pretty close to where they went every time they left the fire base. The Viet Cong and North Vietnamese army units in his area of operation also learned to respect him – and hate him. The fearless black captain who was always out front with his troops, who knew the philosophy of warfare as enunciated by Sun Tzu, fight when you have the numerical advantage, withdraw when you don't, make the enemy fight your battle on your terms, not the other way around as too many U.S. officers did in that war. He lost a few men, but far less than the other company commanders, and pretty soon, the regimental commander was asking for that 'damn snake' Morgan whenever he had a particularly dicey mission. And, Morgan never disappointed him. He'd come away from that first tour with a Silver Star, two Bronze Stars with V-device, indicating they were for service under actual enemy fire, and a Purple Heart from a rifle propelled grenade that exploded near the rim of a ditch he was crouched in, calling artillery fire on a VC position.

With the news of a possible Soviet move on Dagastan, Morgan went into war mode. He was comfortable there. And, despite the fact that only Raine, Duggan, and Jeffers had any military experience, the other employees of the embassy took to his leadership style. His cool, even cheerful demeanor gave them comfort. His almost cocky self-assurance made them think that he knew what he was doing and that he'd take care of them.

That was the effect he desired and anticipated, and getting it from a bunch of civilians made him happier than normal.

"Morning, Mary," he said as he breezed into the executive suite. "How are you this fine morning?"

Mary Sung looked up from the document she'd been typing, her brown face impassive, and her brown, almond shaped eyes calm. "Well, as long as no one shoots at my house, or tries to blow up the embassy; which hasn't happened so far; I guess I'm okay."

For all her Oriental inscrutability, she had a wry sense of humor, which Morgan also appreciated.

"You want a cup of coffee?" she asked. "I just brewed a fresh pot."

"That would be great. I have yet to teach my cook how to make a proper pot of coffee."

A flicker of a smile creased her face. "I've seen the stuff your cook puts on the table. The coffee's probably the most palatable thing on the menu."

True, Morgan thought. Karislov the elderly houseman, cum cook, had worked for his two immediate predecessors, and had never learned to make a proper American meal. They, though, had been married, and their wives did most of the family cooking, using the cook mainly for chopping, cleaning and serving. Morgan, being single, didn't have that option, and the dining out choices in Kazbektun were strictly limited. He didn't have the heart to dismiss the man. He tried hard; Morgan had to give him credit for that. Besides, with the dismal state of Dagastan's economy, it was hardly likely at his age he'd be able to find another job, so Morgan just grimaced and ate the runny eggs, overcooked toast, and slimy bacon. Karislov never seemed to notice the grimace, probably figuring it was the way Morgan smiled.

"Yeah, it can be kind of hard to swallow at times," he said. "Thank goodness for the DATT support flights. I think sometimes I live on peanut butter and crackers. Anything interesting in the overnight traffic?"

Sung would have gone through the cables and dispatches sent to the executive suite from communications, marking for his attention any that were really important, and placing the rest on the bottom of the pile.

"No, nothing to speak of," she said, but there was a kind of hesitation in her voice.

"Then, why is it I sense there *is* something you want to speak of?"

She looked down at her tiny hands resting on the old manual typewriter keyboard. When she looked up, Morgan saw a glistening in her eyes. Damn, he thought, she looks like she wants to cry.

"Oh, David," she said. "I don't know how to say this. . . I mean . . . well, it's not the traffic. I got a call from a friend of mine who works as a secretary in personnel in the Department."

"Are they screwing with your next assignment?"

"No, the call wasn't about me. Kerry; that's my friend; says . . . well, it was about you."

"Really? And, what were the pinheads in personnel saying about me?"

She clasped her hands and took a deep breath. "Kerry says they plan to have the bureau call you back to Washington for consultations, only it won't really be for consultation."

"Come again? How can consultation not be consultation?"

"It was that bitch, Vera Cotton," she said. There was naked fury in her voice when she said the woman's name. "She told them that Ambassador Ellingsworth's death was your fault. They're forming a board of inquiry or something like that, to examine the incident. You're being set up to take the blame."

The glistening in her eyes had formed into two little narrow pools of tears now that perched on the edge of her lower lid. She wiped them away with the back of her hand.

"Kerry said the guy in personnel who's been charged with putting it together objected, but was overruled by someone more senior."

"Well," he said. "I can't really say I'm surprised. I guess in a way I am responsible. I should have been more forceful in getting him to curb his activities, and maybe he'd still be alive."

He didn't say that he thought Ellingsworth had arranged the abortive ambush and had just been unlucky enough to be in the path of a stray bullet. He wasn't sure he'd say that to any board of inquiry either.

"What are you going to do?" Sung asked.

"Right now, what I planned to do when I came in this morning. Try and keep control of things in the embassy. When I go home tonight, I'll pack a ready bag, so when the word's given I can move. Would you do me a favor? Call Montgomery and ask him to have the travel clerk book an open flight to DC for me. Tell him I might be traveling on short notice."

She shook her head. "How can you take this so calmly?"

"Freaking out won't change things, and it could cause you to make a mistake. Things unfold in their own time, and in their own way. If you're calm, maybe you can see where they're going a fraction of a second before they do, so you don't get run over by them."

"And, they say we Chinese are inscrutable. That's the most . . . you sure you aren't a reincarnated Samurai or maybe a Shaolin monk?"

Morgan laughed. "Hell, no; just a guy who's survived combat and who learned his lessons well."

She was still chuckling when he went into his office and started plowing through the stack of paper in his in tray.

He hadn't gotten a tenth of the way down in the stack of cables, memoranda and bulletins before realizing that Mary Sung, as usual, was right. There was nothing of importance. A couple of cables from Washington requesting the embassy to deliver demarches on the local government – one in particular on getting the local views on a law of the seabed treaty struck him as a prime example of the scattershot approach headquarters' staffs took to things. Stuck in the middle of the central Siberian plains, without a body of water larger than a decent sized stock pond on a Texas ranch, Dagastan could care less what the rest of the world did with the bottom of oceans its people could never see. But, someone somewhere wanted the information, so some mid-level officer drafted the instruction, had some secretary type it up, and then submitted it to a senior supervisor for clearance and transmittal approval. With everything that was happening, Morgan thought it an incredible waste of resources to have people spend time doing mindless things like this, but he'd instruct Dennis Larson to get it done anyway. *You have to feed the beast,* he thought, *or it will devour you.*

He'd just about made it to the bottom of the pile when Mary Sung stuck her head around the door frame. "Dave, Carlton and the colonel are here to see you," she said, and ducked back out of sight.

Raine and Duggan, dressed in wrinkled green utility uniforms, the kind Morgan remembered as army fatigues, without name tags or rank insignia, and coated with a patina of dust, walked in. They looked haggard, but were smiling.

"Okay, whose canary did you two cats eat?" Morgan asked.

The pulled up chairs in front of his desk. Duggan leaned forward, his beefy hands scattering dust on the polished wood surface.

"Me and Blood here decided to do a little front line reconnaissance," he said. "Paid off, too."

Morgan cocked his head, looking at the colonel, but said nothing.

"Gonna make us tell you, eh?" Raine asked. "Dang, compadre, if you're not a cold one. Okay, Pat, might as well tell him. You're better with that military jargon than I am, so you go ahead."

"We went over to the western border area," Duggan said. There was a note of excitement in his voice. "Got up real close, too, and the reports are true. Ivan's got main battle tank units right up against the border so close you could throw rocks at 'em. Lots of motorized infantry as well, and they don't look like they're exercising. These guys look loaded for bear."

"I have to agree," Raine said. "If I had to guess, I'd say they're set to move in a day or two at most."

"What are our Dagastani friends doing about it?" Morgan asked.

"Mostly gettin' the hell out of the way," Duggan said. "Border posts are lightly manned. Nothing but a few guys with AKs. No armor to support 'em, not that it would matter. It wouldn't take much more than a tank regiment and a couple of good motorized infantry regiments to overrun this place in the time it takes them to drive from the western to the eastern border."

"The Dagastani army's that bad?"

"Worse. They were never much use for anything other than keeping the population in line and guarding the head man's house and office."

Raine laughed harshly. "And, they didn't do too good a job at the latter. Look at how easily Dragov took over."

Morgan pulled a note pad from his desk drawer and began taking notes. This would have to be reported to Washington immediately. There was no time to get Larson briefed in, so he'd write the cable himself. It would be short and to the point.

"Do you think there'll be much violence and bloodshed?" he asked the two men.

"Nah," Duggan said, shaking his head. "These guys ain't stupid. They're not about to go up against an army that can crush them before lunch. I think it'll be a quick and painless takeover."

"Agreed," Raine said. "Question is; what happens after they take over. I can't imagine they're too happy with Dragov for trying to cozy up to us. Kovasc was their man for years, someone they could depend on. We might see a few more unexplained disappearances."

Morgan scribbled that latter note and then underlined it. He was already composing the message in his mind: a smooth takeover by Soviet forces, but likely to be some violence behind closed doors as the Russians 'readjusted' Dagastan's national policy and leadership. Oh, that would get the bureaucracy's wheels spinning for sure, he thought. Nothing gets a bureaucracy's attention like a crisis. Problem was, though, Washington already had a number of crises to deal with, and in Morgan's experience, it had never been able to deal effectively with more than one large and one small crisis at a time. Things were about to get interesting.

Chapter Twelve

Friday, June 27, 1975, Dagastan

Dagastan is far enough north that during the summer months the dawn comes early. It's usually light enough out to read by three in the morning. Not that the two young Dagastani border guards, members of the Rus ethnic group who'd been in the unit only six months before being assigned duty at this lonely outpost, had time or inclination to read.

They're main objective was to stay awake. The sergeant in charge of the sector had an unfortunate habit of surprise inspections at odd hours, and the penalty for being caught asleep on post was severe. Not that it made any difference. Out this far west, there were few border crossers other than the occasional smuggler of Russian goods into Dagastan's hungry, impoverished market.

Even though it was almost the middle of summer, up here, straddling the Arctic Circle, it was cold at three in the morning. Cold enough to cause the guards to be able to see the vapor from their breathing, white billows that poured from their noses and mouths as they stood shivering near the little paraffin tin that was their only source of heat.

It had been a quiet night. Not even the sound of night birds disturbed them. The area was barren and sterile, with little sustenance for any creature. The only sound had been the moaning of the wind coming from the north over the mountains, a wind that was laden with the chill of the deep, forbidding arctic ice.

Huddled over the small stove, they hadn't bothered to scan the area outside the small hut in which they alternately sat and stood guard. They were, thus, surprised when the hut started trembling. The very ground around them seemed to be undulating like ocean swells. And, the noise. The noise was deafening. It was like an avalanche that happens suddenly in the narrow mountain passes, that catches you unawares just before burying you under tons of rock. The two border guards looked at each other, eyes wide. Whether it was uncertainty, puzzlement of fear, or perhaps a mixture of all three, they probably could not have said – if, in fact, they'd been able to speak at all at that moment.

Finally, the older of the two, older by a mere two years, decided to stand and look out the small, fly-specked window of the hut to see what was making such a ruckus. When he did, he froze; his face rigid in a look of terror and bemusement. His companion, looking up from where he squatted on the dirt floor, still warming his hands over the heater, saw the look on his face.

"What is it Vladim?" he asked.

"Muh-, muh-," was all the stunned man could get out.

"By your mother, Vladim," the younger man said as he stood and dusted off his trousers. "Sometimes you can be so - -"

He too went into a state of semi-shock, his lips moving, but no sound issuing forth. His brain refused at first to believe what his eyes were seeing and what his ears were hearing.

"Mother of God," the older guard finally got out. "Would you look at that!"

He crossed himself, praying silently to the Blessed Virgin to be shown mercy, and wishing a priest was present because he feared he would die without the last rites being properly administered.

What lay before their incredulous eyes was designed to impress; to impress and intimidate.

A line of ten Soviet T-55 main battle tanks, painted gleaming white, their main gun turrets jutting forward, bore down upon the two hapless guards. Behind the tanks came two columns of five dull green BTR-70 armored personnel carriers with PKT machine guns mounted on turrets atop their flat boat-shaped bodies. The turrets of the tanks, and the eight big rubber tires of each APC, tore up the earth and kicked up a cloud of dust behind the formation that billowed as it rose more than fifty feet into the early morning air.

The sound of twenty heavy duty engines was deafening in the morning air, getting louder as they drew nearer. The ground shook. The two border guards stood stiffly, shaking in their boots.

Ten yards from the swing pole that was placed across the dirt road leading from the Russian side of the border into Dagastan, the column came to a clanking, grinding halt, throwing bits of dust and gravel against the window of the hut.

As the dust settled, a Soviet officer, a captain by the look of the crimson shoulder board with the single red stripe up the middle and the five small gold stars, came out of one of the APCs and walked between two of the tanks toward the barrier. When he reached the barrier he stopped and looked around.

In Russian, he called, "Who is on duty here? Come out and present yourself."

His tone was commanding. Well it could be, the guards thought, with so much fire power at his shoulder. The two guards inched slowly out of the hut.

"We are on duty, comrade," Vladim, the older guard said. "What can we do for you?"

"You can lift this barrier so that we may pass," the officer said, as he looked down his razor sharp nose at them.

Vladim looked around. Except for the barrier, a flimsy wooden pole on a swivel that rested at the other end in a metal fork set in a concrete slab. There was no fence. After all, the only neighbor Dagastan had was Russia, and they were fraternal allies. The damn tanks only had to drive to the right and left and they'd pass the border post as if it wasn't there. Yet, there was something in the officer's voice that told the guards that they'd better comply with his order. Vladim jerked his head at his young companion and ran to the pivot end of the barrier. His comrade ran to the other end and removed the leather loop that kept the barrier from swinging up until it was desired for it to rise. As he loosened the tether, the pole, weighted at the pivot end with a large block of cement, began to rise. Vladim guided it so it would rise at a steady rate rather than simply flipping up. The sergeant was picky about such things. The barrier had to be raised properly. After all, this was the first sight many people had of the country, and they had to make a good impression. When the barrier was as far up as it could go – still not high enough or out of the way for a tank to pass between without clipping it – Vladim and his colleague stood aside, facing each other and saluted.

"Comrade Captain," Vladim said. "The barrier is raised."

The Soviet officer sloppily returned their salutes and returned to his vehicle behind the tanks. Shortly, the roar of engines resumed and the vehicles began moving forward, diverging as they neared the customs hut, with half passing to the left and half to the right.

"Fuck your mother," Vladim said as the last BTR-70 clanked past. "Those sons of dogs didn't even go through the barrier. Why, I wonder, did that bastard have us raise it."

"Probably just because he could," his young companion said.

As the dust settled, the lowered the barrier back into position and resumed their sentry duty, waiting for the sergeant to come and relieve them. At that time, they would have an interesting story to tell.

It took five hours for the Soviet column, moving completely unopposed, sometimes on the roads and sometimes cutting across fields, chewing up the crops growing in them, to reach the outskirts of Kazbektun. A frightened flow of refugees, the few peasants who'd gotten wind of its approach in enough time to throw families and meager possessions in trucks, if they had them, and flee toward the city, preceded the tanks and APCs. Those without trucks simply cowered in their huts until the behemoth had passed.

At five past eight, the lead tank sat on a rise with a view down the slope at Kazbektun huddled in the valley before them. The road from this point was paved, although it was more pothole than pavement.

A signal was passed, and the tanks moved out to the flanks, while the APCs moved into position between them, and the procession began a slow, stately parade down the incline toward the city.

The first person to see the Soviets who wasn't so scared he was unable to do anything but cross himself and mutter was a stringer for BBC who had managed to get a visa to come to Dagastan to do a series of human interest pieces on the country's efforts to modernize. He was shocked at what he was seeing, but had been around long enough to recognize Soviet military hardware, and had the presence of mind to use the tiny Minolta to snap a few shots before scurrying back into an alley to make his way to the British embassy. He carried the Minolta to get pictures of people without freaking them out, or having them even knowing their pictures were being taken. It was sometimes used, cupping it next to his thigh, to take photos of military and government installations without the guards being aware. What he had now, he knew, would make his reputation.

The next rational person to get wind of the Soviets' arrival was a young US Marine corporal from Texas named Kellogg, who was standing first watch at Post One at the American embassy. The first indication that all was not as it should be was an increase in the flow of people on the street that passed in front of the embassy; the upsurge was all one way, from west to east, and most of the traffic was of a type, country folks with possessions piled in the back of rusty old trucks. Kellogg made a mental note of the phenomenon and turned his attention back to the sidewalk and the line of people on it waiting to get into the consular section to apply for a visa. There'd been an increase there, too, he noted, but that crowd represented a broad swath of Dagastani society. His job was to keep the embassy – primarily the classified documents and equipment, secondarily the people working inside – safe. Beneath the counter of the metal-reinforced booth in which he worked behind a sheet of thick, bullet proof glass, was a riot shotgun and several canisters of CS, a particularly noxious tear gas that burned like hell when it hit your skin or eyes. He knew because in training everyone had to expose themselves to the stuff so they knew its effects. On his hip he carried a regulation .45 caliber automatic with a ten-round magazine inside and two extra magazines on his belt, a short-range handheld radio for use when he was away from his station checking the other embassy spaces, and a PR-24 side-handle baton or nightstick made of hard wood. Corporal Kellogg was equipped to handle every conceivable emergency the embassy might face short of a nuclear attack. Or, he thought he was. The sight of a white Russian T-55 tank trundling past the front of the embassy, though, wasn't in any of the emergency scenarios he'd been taught.

He blinked at the first one, thinking perhaps he might be hallucinating. But, when the second passed, followed by a big green armored personnel carrier with a soldier in dull green uniform manning the machine gun mounted on its top, he knew he wasn't dreaming – he was having a nightmare.

But, Corporal Roy Lee Kellogg from Henderson, Texas, had faced down wounded panthers in the woods hunting as a boy, and had gone through some of the toughest training the Marine Corps had to offer. He didn't panic, even when he knew he was in the middle of a bad dream turned to worse reality. He calmly picked up the phone and dialed the regional security officer's extension.

"RSO's office, Jeffers here," Pete Jeffers' reassuring voice came through the earpiece.

"RSO, this here's Corporal Kellogg at Post One. I think y'all better come up here and take a look at what's happenin' out in the street, 'cause if I try to tell you, you might think I been drinkin' on duty."

Jeffers knew his marines didn't drink on duty, so he broke the connection and ran flat out from his office at the rear of the embassy, down on the level that was below ground in the front of the building, but that let out into a wide parking lot and storage area in the back, to Post One. He arrived just as a tank and two APCs were roaring past, and like Corporal Kellogg, he at first thought he might be hallucinating, but the smell of exhaust fumes and the ear-punishing roar of the engines told him otherwise.

Jeffers went inside the booth with the marine and picked up the phone. He dialed David Morgan's office.

"Front office, charge's secretary," Mary Sung said. "How may I help you?"

"Mary, it's Pete Jeffers. Put Dave on please."

A short pause, and, "What is it, Pete?" Morgan's deep voice was somehow reassuring to the young security officer.

"Dave, the Russians have landed," was all that Jeffers could think to say.

Chapter Thirteen

It didn't take long for the news to spread through the city. Thanks to Morgan's people and an enterprising BBC stringer, it spread through the diplomatic community like a Texas grass fire in the middle of a rainless July.

Almost as soon as he'd broken the connection with Jeffers, Morgan got a call from the British ambassador, Gavin McLeod, a dour Scot with a fondness for vodka, asking if he could come immediately to the British residence to discuss the developing security situation.

Morgan arrived at the stately mansion that Her Majesty's Government had completely refitted for their representative some twenty minutes later. McLeod's residence sat on a hill even higher than the one the American ambassador's house was on, giving a commanding view of all of Kazbektun and the steppes and hills all around. A majestic, curving white stone drive wound up from the large wrought iron entry gate and under a large *porte cochere* in front of marble steps leading up to a set of double doors of dark brown wood with brass door handles and fittings, and a door knocker that was a lion's head with a brass ring in its mouth.

Several other cars were already parked in the macadam-covered parking area to the left of the entrance. A Dagastani man wearing a stiff looking black suit over a shirt with a high white collar answered the door. He bowed and escorted Morgan through the large representational area to a patio where four dour looking men were sitting around a large glass topped wrought iron table sipping some brown liquid that Morgan took to be tea.

McLeod, with a shock of slightly rumpled white hair, was wearing a dark suit with some kind of regimental tie, as usual. He stood when David came out on to the patio and came over to shake his hand.

"David, so glad you could make it," he said. "Do come and join us. Would you like a cup of tea?"

Morgan nodded. He wasn't a big tea drinker, but, when in Rome and all that, he thought. Besides, the tea wasn't all that bad. He walked around the table, greeting and shaking hands with the others. Henri Jean Langlois, the French ambassador, was a portly, ruddy cheeked Parisian whose English was so heavily accented it was almost tiring to engage him in conversation. Jacob Treworthy, a Canadian from the far west of his country, was the Canadian ambassador. He was tall and gaunt, with dark brown hair that kept falling over his forehead. Morgan thought that if the man grew a beard he'd look like Abraham Lincoln. Knowing Canadian sensitivities, though, he never said so aloud. Finally, there was George Linville, a brash Australian who, before joining the Australian diplomatic service had been a cattle rancher in the outback. Morgan's height and build, he had the healthy look of someone who spends a lot of time outside and who exercises frequently. Morgan knew and got along with him better than the other three.

As he sat and took a sip of the pungent, strong tea – he drew a mildly rebuking look from Langlois when he drank it without milk or sugar – McLeod resumed his place at the table and tapped the side of his cup with a small silver spoon.

"Gentlemen," he said. "Now that we're all here, I suppose I should explain why I asked for this impromptu meeting."

There were nods around the table.

"I assume zis ees regarding zee presence of

our Russian friends," Langlois said.

"Yes it is, Henri," McLeod said. "And, what we five plan to do about it."

"What the hell *can* we do about it, mate," Linville said, winking at Morgan over the edge of his cup. "The bloody bastards are here. Other than report it to our respective capitals and then spend our time answering bloody stupid questions from them, there don't seem to be a lot we can do."

Morgan restrained himself from smiling in agreement. McLeod and Linville were often at odds with each other; not exactly enemies, but McLeod, despite being Scot, had a very English sense of decorum which the Aussie, in his view, lacked. He did think, though, that as blunt and undiplomatic as he might be, Linville had made a valid point.

"I'm afraid, Gavin, that I must agree with George," he said in a measured, unemotional tone. "I don't know about the rest of you, but we've been getting hints for days of a possible Soviet move. We reported it to Washington, but received no instructions, just, as George says; questions. Now that they're here, we'll need to find out as much as we can about their intentions, but, beyond that, there's not much we can do."

McLeod didn't look happy to have reality dashed in his face like that. Likely, Morgan thought, he felt that they *ought* to be able to do something, that their respective governments expected them to do something, and the fact that he really couldn't do anything was unsettling. Morgan knew that there were those in Washington who, despite knowing he was powerless to do much beyond report on events, would pressure him to *do* something. McLeod sighed and slumped his shoulders.

"I know you're both right," he said. "It's just very frustrating."

"Well, we can attempt to contact the foreign ministry to see if we can get a sense of what's what," Treworthy said, brushing hair from his broad forehead.

"Capital idea that, Jacob," McLeod said. "Certainly beats sitting around twiddling our fingers, what? Of course, we also need to coordinate our emergency actions, just in case things get ugly." He looked around the table inquiringly.

"We're not doing much different than we normally do," Morgan said. "My guys have a sense that, while the Soviets aren't all that well disposed toward us, their presence actually minimizes the risk of violence."

"*Certainment*," Langlois said. "I am in agreement wiz David, *completment*. I sink zee Russians will keep order."

There were nods around the table, but McLeod still frowned. "I don't disagree," he said. "But, I think prudence dictates that we prepare for the worse case." He looked at Morgan. "Dave, I'm assuming your air force people out of Germany are closest to us?"

"Probably," Morgan replied. "Although, we have forces in Japan and Korea that could probably get here as quickly, and they wouldn't have to fly past Moscow to do it. I'll get on to Washington to look at possibilities and get back to you guys."

"That would be fine. I'm afraid Her Majesty's forces are rather thin on the ground in this part of the world, and our heavy lift capacity is not what it needs to be."

Meaning, Morgan thought, that as usual, it was up to the good old U. S. of A to pull everyone's asses out of the fire if someone lit it. Some things just never change.

They spent a few more minutes comparing notes on what each knew about the situation and agreeing to meet regularly at McLeod's residence to keep each other informed. Morgan would rather have been doing something else than sitting around nattering with a bunch of powerless diplomats, but he understood the need to maintain relationships.

Back at the embassy, he had Sung call Larson, Jeffers, Raine, and Duggan to his office.

When they were all settled around the table in the corner and coffee had been poured, he filled them in on his meeting with the other ambassadors.

"So," Raine said. "As usual, they're waiting to see what we'll do."

"They do have a point, though," Duggan said. "We're the only nation with the ability to project into this region. If it comes to an emergency evacuation, they have to rely on us."

"Which brings me to the question of whether we'd get support from EUCOM or PACOM," Morgan said, referring to the US European and Pacific military commands.

"Good question," Duggan said. "The units in Germany are set up to support us for a NEO." He referred to a noncombatant evacuation, when the US military removes civilians from a dangerous area. "But, if we're having problems with the Russkies, they might have a problem getting overflight clearance from Germany, providing the Germans would even approve them taking off if they feared it might piss Ivan off. PACOM's units are closer. They can stage out of Japan or Korea, and both of those countries are likely to approve such operations. The problem would be them having to fly awful close to the damn North Korean border if they're to take the shortest routes."

"In other words," Morgan said. "It's a crap

shoot. We could find ourselves stuck here."

Duggan shrugged.

"My guys are telling me that things are quiet in town," Jeffers said. "So far, the Russians haven't done much beyond put tanks and troops in front of key installations. It might just be wishful thinking on my part, but I don't think it'll come to an evacuation."

"I concur," Raine said. "The Russians don't give a fig about us. They're here to sort the locals out, and that shouldn't be much of a problem. Hell, they rolled in here from the border without a finger being lifted to stop them, or even slow them down."

"For the record, I agree," Morgan said. "But, we'll have to deal with a possible knee jerk reaction from Washington to have us prepare to get out of Dodge." He turned to Larson. "Dennis, get to working on a cable letting them know things are quiet and that we'll keep them advised." He handed him the notes of his meeting with the other ambassadors. "Insert this information as appropriate, and make sure you include our embassies in London, Paris, Ottawa and Canberra as info addressees. If there's nothing else, let's get to work. Keep me posted as you learn things. I'll call a general staff meeting in a bit to fill everyone else in and keep people from panicking."

Everyone nodded and hustled off to do their

jobs. Morgan remained at the table, sipping his coffee and making notes he'd use at the general meeting. When he'd finished, he called Sung in and directed her to set up a meeting for the entire American staff in the conference room.

When he arrived at the conference room, it was already crowded, with people standing along the walls. Every seat around the big table was filled except for his seat nearest the door. Despite him telling them it was unnecessary for them to stand each time he entered the room, when he walked in, everyone stood. As he looked around, he noted that except for Mary Sung and the four officers he'd just spoken with, everyone else had nervous looks.

He waved them to their seats and sat, pulling out his notes. In an even tone, he outlined what they knew of the situation, gave a brief summary of his meeting with the other ambassadors, and assured them that the embassy was in no danger. Whether it was his own calmness, or just that nothing serious had happened – beyond the arrival of a large armed contingent of Soviets – but, quickly the mood softened. Tension dropped noticeably. When he went around the room to ask for questions or comments, no one spoke. They just nodded. A couple of the junior officers smiled. Morgan knew what they were thinking. Finally, they were experiencing real world diplomacy. It would be something to make conversation about at cocktail receptions for the rest of their careers.

Satisfied that the situation inside the embassy was under control, he dismissed everyone and, with Sung walking beside him, headed back to his office.

They were both surprised to see a strange man in a slightly rumpled suit, with two large suitcases on the floor at his feet, sitting on the visitor's chair near Sung's desk. When they entered the executive area, the man rose and stuck out his hand.

"David," he said. "I'm Montgomery Jackson-Leigh, just call me Monty. Can we go into your office and talk privately?"

As Morgan shook the man's hand, he thought the name was familiar, but couldn't place it. Beside him, he sensed Sung tensing. She had a stricken look on her face.

"Sure," he said. "Mary, could you bring some fresh coffee?"

Chapter Fourteen

"Do I know you?" Morgan asked.

The sudden appearance of this stranger; a man who seemed totally at home and, in fact, in command of the situation, was a bit unnerving, and his inability to place the name and face was frankly annoying.

"We've never formally met," the stranger said. "I wasn't posted to my current job until after you were assigned here."

Jackson-Leigh walked over to the little table in the corner and sat without being invited. Another thing that annoyed Morgan; that, and the fact that he'd sat in the chair facing in, the chair that Morgan usually used, with his back to his host.

"I'm the DAS for the bureau covering this part of the world," Jackson-Leigh went on, looking over his shoulder at Morgan.

"Are you here on vacation?" Morgan asked. "This is a hell of a place to be doing that, and now, quite frankly, is not the best time."

"No, David, I'm here on official business."

Morgan felt his cheeks go hot. He walked around and stood looking down at his visitor.

"Then, you want to tell me why the hell I didn't get a request for country clearance?"

This was over the top. No government employee enters a country on official business without obtaining country clearance from the embassy in that country; or in other words, the ambassador or charge d'affaires.

Jackson-Leigh's cheeks flushed, and he looked down at the table top. Well, Morgan thought, at least the son of a bitch has the decency to be embarrassed.

"I know I should have done that," Jackson-Leigh said. "But, I wanted to be able to talk to you face-to-face without anything clouding the conversation. If I'd requested country clearance, I would have to have explained the reason for my visit or lied. I didn't want to do either."

Mary Sung brought a pot of coffee and two fresh mugs in. She put them on the table in front of Jackson-Leigh, and with a glance at Morgan, padded soundlessly out. Morgan sat.

He poured a mug of coffee for his guest, and then one for himself.

"Okay," he said after taking a sip. "I'm willing to let you explain to me why you've violated every procedure in the book. Why does a deputy assistant secretary have to sneak into a shithole like Dagastan in the first place?"

Jackson-Leigh's cheeks flushed a darker color.

"They told me you were quite blunt," he said. "You were in the army, weren't you?"

"Yeah," Morgan said.

"That explains the language. I'm not used to hearing senior officers in your position use such coarse and vulgar language. But, I guess when you were in the army, you heard far worse."

Oh, Lord, Morgan thought, *another stick up his ass Puritan who probably says 'shoot' instead of 'shit,' and who has a BM, if he even refers to bodily functions.* He tried to keep his expression impassive. Since he joined the Foreign Service, he had almost become accustomed to the offhand comments about military people, and how strange they are, from his colleagues, many of whom had come straight from college to the service, and had never served a day in uniform, not even the Boy Scouts.

"Yeah," he said evenly. "I've heard worse.

But, back to my question. Why are you here?"

The question, asked again, just as bluntly as the first time, seemed to catch the man off guard. He fiddled momentarily with his fingers, and then finally, looked at Morgan. There was something unreadable in his dark brown eyes.

"Look, Dave; you don't mind if I call you Dave, do you?" Morgan shrugged. "Okay, it's like this. The bureau has been asked to summon you back to Washington, and they've sent me here to fill in for you while you're gone. I didn't want you getting this cold in a cable or an impersonal phone call, so I broke the travel rules to be able to tell you to your face."

"What's the big deal? I'm just the DCM, filling in temporarily until they can find a new ambassador. Given my rank, and the time it seems to be taking for them to find someone, it doesn't surprise me they'd be sending someone out. But, why do I have to be recalled? Why not just step back down to my DCM job?"

"Uh, well . . . it's . . . not as simple as that. Hell, I might as well level with you. You're not being called back for consultations; not as such at least. Personnel has been directed to inquire into the circumstances of Ambassador Ellingsworth's death, and you're the star witness. They actually want you back for that, but they didn't want to put it in a formal document. You understand how these things work?"

He did, and he didn't. Morgan was quite familiar with the bureaucracy's tendency to find a downhill direction for the shit to flow, but he didn't understand why they'd want to keep it quiet that they were investigating the death of a senior official. After all his years in the service they could still surprise him sometimes.

"Okay, so I go back to Washington to give my testimony to some departmental committee, and then back here, right? How long do you think that might take?"

"That's hard to say. It could be a few days or a few weeks. These boards work at their own pace, so it's best to err on the side of it taking longer than you anticipate. My advice would be to plan for an extended stay in DC. You can have a few days to pack and leave if you need it."

Morgan felt the beginning of white hot anger. So, they were planning to throw him to the sharks, were they? For all his act of consideration; coming to deliver bad news in person rather than have it sent by cable or phone, Jackson-Leigh was as much a bureaucratic 'cover your ass' type as the nameless, faceless ones who were planning to sit in judgment on him. And, he was convinced that sticking it to him for Ellingsworth's death was precisely what they planned to do.

So be it. You want a piece of Dave Morgan's ass, you'd better bring your lunch, 'cause I don't plan to roll over and play dead. "Actually," he said. "I won't need any time at all. I got wind I'd probably be called back, so I packed a ready bag and had open flight reservations made. I can be out of here tonight."

He stood and walked out of his office, leaving Montgomery Jackson-Leigh, the new charge d'affaires, sitting there with his mouth open.

Chapter Fifteen

Tuesday – Wednesday, July 1 – 2, 1975,
Dagastan to Washington, DC

The only delay Morgan made before leaving the embassy was to tell Mary Sung to inform the staff he was leaving, and apologize for his not saying a proper farewell to everyone, but he felt they'd understand given the circumstances.

Pete Jeffers and Carlton Raine arrived at his residence only minutes behind him as he was wrestling his two suitcases toward the front door with the help of the houseman, who looked puzzled that he was leaving so suddenly, despite having seen the packed bags for a few days.

Morgan ordered the two not to go with him to the airport, over their strong objections. He valued their friendship, but wanted to put things behind him as quickly as possible. The future was murky, so there was no reason to be burdened by the past as you tried to navigate through it. His last words to the two of them, before he got into his car for that final ride to the airport was to 'take care of yourselves and each other, and try and keep the new guy out of trouble.'

The ordinary routing for embassy personnel was to take a Lufthansa flight from Kazbektun to Frankfurt and then switch to Northwest for the flight to Dulles International Airport in Virginia just outside Washington. The Frankfurt flight, though, didn't depart until midnight, and Morgan had no taste for waiting in Kazbektun's airport any longer than necessary. Fortunately for him his travel clerk had good relations with the country manager for KLM and he was able to get a late afternoon KLM flight to Amsterdam, with the added bonus of an overnight stay courtesy of the airlines, with a connection the next day at midday to Dulles.

The flight to Amsterdam's Schiphol Airport was long and boring. Morgan killed time by flipping through the KLM in-flight magazine. It was early evening when they landed, and this far north, the sun was still up, would in fact still be up until well after nine pm. He'd checked his bags through to Washington, keeping just a small carry-on with clean underwear and his toiletries, and with his diplomatic passport, he breezed through customs and immigration and took a taxi to the nearby airport hotel. He presented the airline voucher and was given a ground floor room that had a view of the airport. He pulled the curtains shut, but the penetrating rays of the sun, which was still a hand's width from the horizon, lit up the room like noon.

Knowing he'd be unable to get to sleep until it got dark, he washed his face and went out front of the hotel and found a taxi driver who spoke passable English, though with a thick accent, and asked where he could go to unwind for a few hours.

With a wink and a knowing smile the driver said, "Not to vorry, I know chust the place."

The drive from the airport area to what Morgan took to be the center of Amsterdam didn't take long. The driver pulled to the curb in an area of winding streets and ancient looking buildings that leaned in every direction. The sidewalks were filled with people; couples holding hands or fondling each other, tour groups, and even a few family groups with what appeared to be pre-teen children. The tour groups and families were stopping frequently and pointing at the windows of some of the buildings. It didn't take Morgan long to see why. In several of the buildings, women of many different races, dressed in scanty costumes sat in red-fringe-lined spaces like miniature parlors, beckoning passersby, and it wasn't left to the imagination why they beckoned.

Damn, he thought, I heard Amsterdam had a red light district, but this takes the cake. At least it's truth in advertising, I suppose. You get to window shop before you buy. He wasn't in the market, though, so he walked on, only occasionally glancing in the direction of a window display.

Near the end of the block, he saw a sign over a door that read *Kaffe*, which he assumed meant either coffee or café, so he went in. It was, in fact, a bar, serving all kinds of beer and liquor. He took a table in the corner to the right of the door, and when the buxom, blonde waitress came over, ordered a bier. She asked him something in a language that sounded almost like German, but not quite, so he simply nodded and shrugged and said *machs nicht*, which was about all the German he knew, and he wasn't completely sure it really meant 'it doesn't matter.' The waitress, though, smiled at him and walked back to the bar, swinging her ample hips beneath the knee length skirt she wore, and returned soon with a large clear glass mug full of amber liquid with a nice frothy head. He took a sip. It wasn't bad. A bit bitter, but not bad. He'd changed some dollars for local currency in the airport, so he slid one of the larger notes across the table to her. She shook her head and pulled a smaller note from his hand, and gave him several odd-shaped coins of different sizes in change. Not bad, and not too expensive either. He sat back and sipped, watching the ebb and flow of customers in the place.

By the time he'd finished his beer, he could see through the small plate glass window that the sky was darker. The street lights provided most of the illumination. So, he went outside, found a taxi and went back to his hotel.

After a shave and shower, he fell across the double bed and slept until nearly nine the next morning.

He ate a light breakfast and killed time sitting in his room watching TV. There was one English channel, but it showed mostly British TV shows, which he had a hard time following. There was a Dutch channel that showed ads and movies that would have been more appropriate in the red light district, so he flipped quickly past it. No sense getting all worked up, he thought. It's a long flight with nowhere to go.

Finally, about four hours before his flight time, he checked out and took a taxi back to the airport.

He killed some more time by walking through the terminal shops, again shocked that some of them sold pornographic magazines and sex toys right out in the open. By the time he made his way to his departure gate, he'd decided that the rumors he'd heard about Amsterdam were true – it certainly seemed to be a city where anything and everything goes.

The crew on the KLM flight to Washington was about evenly divided between European and American stewardesses, and Morgan lucked out and got an American serving in his part of the cabin. Not that it mattered, because immediately after eating the light supper that was the first inflight meal, he leaned his seat back and fell asleep instantly.

He woke up when he felt a change in the plane's movement, indicating that they were descending. The pilot's voice announced in Dutch, German, French and English that they were making their final approach into Dulles International Airport, Washington, DC. He'd slept most of the eight-hour flight.

The landing was smooth, but the ride from the outer terminal by bus to the little side door at the main terminal through which international passengers had to go for immigration formalities was bumpy. The lines of American citizens and green card holders were long, and the bored-looking immigration officers moved like they were being paid by the hour, which is almost how long it took him to get through to baggage claim to retrieve his two suitcases. Another long wait to go through customs, and then outside the terminal he got a taxi and asked to be taken to the Francis Scott Key Hotel on Twentieth Street in DC. A long-stay hotel frequented by State Department employees in the area temporarily, it offered a small efficiency suite for eighteen dollars a night. That kept him within the per diem rates, which were good for sixty days, and he certainly hoped he wouldn't be in the city that long.

He was assigned a unit with a view to the north, mostly the other three, four, and five story buildings on the street. It was almost seven in the evening, but having slept on the plane, he didn't feel sleepy, so he decided to leave his unpacking for later, and walk down toward the National Mall to get a look at the monuments after dark, when they're all lit up.

About the time Morgan arrived in front of the Lincoln Memorial, an American Airlines jet from Miami was landing at nearby National Airport. Among the passengers getting off was a man in his late sixties, with thin white hair that was combed across the front of his skull to conceal his baldness, wearing an expensive looking pearl gray suit, white silk shirt, and dark blue tie. As he walked through the door into the arrival lounge, he stopped and looked around. He took a deep breath, and smiled, his watery blue eyes shining.

"Oh my, it is so good to be home," Niles Hitchcock said.

Chapter Sixteen

Thursday, July 3, 1975, Washington, DC

Morgan fell into bed after his walk along the Mall, and slept until seven the next morning.

Upon rising, he showered and dug around in his suitcase until he found pants, a shirt, and a jacket that weren't too wrinkled. He dressed and went down to the hotel's little dining room and had his first decent breakfast in three years. After eating, he went back to his room and dialed the number Samuel Gosnell had given him – the direct line to the desk officer's office phone.

"Dagastan desk, Sam Gosnell speaking, how can I help you?" the voice said.

"Dave Morgan here," Morgan said. "I just got into town last night. Do you have any idea what my schedule is."

"Uh, Mr. Morgan, I mean, Dave," Gosnell said. "I didn't expect you to arrive so soon. I figured you'd arrive over the weekend, or even sometime next week. There's nothing scheduled, but if you'll give me your number, I'll check around and let you know."

"Is there any chance anything will be scheduled for today?"

"Not likely," Gosnell said. He laughed. "Just about everyone's trying to get out of here early today to get a jump on the long holiday weekend. I doubt there'll be anything before Monday, and even then it'll probably be light."

"Okay," Morgan said. He gave the number of the hotel's front desk. "I might go out to do some grocery shopping, so just leave a message."

Gosnell agreed, and Morgan put the phone back in the cradle. Satisfied that he wouldn't need to don a tie, he removed the jacket and hung it in the closet. He noticed an iron and ironing board in the back of the closet. After filling the little refrigerator with food and drink, he decided he'd spend the rest of the day ironing the wrinkles out of his clothes and using the hotel's laundry room to clean the items that needed it.

Even though he was getting per diem, it only covered his hotel bill and minimum additional expenses, which meant he'd have to make several trips on foot stocking up on food. Taxi fares could run up fast, and just three or four trips could eat up the miscellaneous expense portion of his per diem payments, which wouldn't be paid until the end of the trip anyway.

As Morgan set out to find local markets and liquor stores, Senator Jonathan Appleby was sitting behind the large oak desk in his office on the second floor of the Russell Senate Office Building just northeast of the Capitol. With this being the last legislative day before the Fourth of July and summer recess, his schedule was uncharacteristically light. There were no pending bills he had to worry about, and his hearing schedule had been cleared except for a couple of nominations that one of his colleagues had put a hold on – for reasons Appleby was determined to learn; right after Labor Day.

He'd let most of his staff take off early to prepare for July Fourth activities, or be with their families. There was just one secretary, a middle-aged, gray haired spinster who'd been with him since he was a state legislator, manning the front desk. With no family, and not being one to enjoy being in crowds, she had no plans, so he didn't feel too guilty about her having to work.

He was just going over his planned activities

back home in North Dakota; mostly grip and grin sessions with local supporters, plus a couple of fund raising events. He'd have time to do some serious fishing this trip. He leaned back in his chair, thinking about standing hip dip in some cold mountain stream, casting his fly far out in hopes of landing a big one.

The clang of the phone on his desk yanked him out of his reverie.

"Yeah, Maggie," he said. "What is it?"

"Senator, there's a man on the phone who won't give his name, but he insists that you'll take his call. He says it's a matter of life or death."

"Sounds like some crackpot to me. Just blow him off, but do it nicely."

"I tried that, sir," she said, with a note of pleading in her voice. "But, he was having none of it. Said to tell you the White Dragon has returned, whatever that means."

Appleby felt a tightening in his chest. It couldn't be, he thought. That son of a bitch knew better than to call him directly, and from Costa Rica at that.

"Okay, Maggie, put him on," he said after he'd calmed his breathing. "And, why don't you take the rest of the day off. I think I'm busting out of here as soon as I get off the phone."

"You sure you don't need me to stay, Senator. I don't mind."

"No, you go on and hightail it out of here. I'll turn off the lights."

He could almost hear her disapproval as she punched the buttons to transfer the call.

"Appleby here," he said. "Who is this?"

The voice he feared, that he hoped wouldn't be on the line, came through crystal clear.

"Jonathan, Niles Hitchcock here. We need to talk."

"What's so important you're making a long distance call, Niles?"

"I'm not calling long distance, Jonathan. I'm at my place in Georgetown. Now, about that conversation; where would you like to meet?"

Chapter Seventeen

Friday, July 4, 1975, Washington, DC

Friday morning dawned bright and clear, with just a hint of moisture in the air, but no real threat of rain. Morgan rose early and, dressed in comfortable clothing, slacks and short sleeve pullover with crepe soled walking shoes, he went downstairs and joined the other early riser residents for breakfast, a sumptuous southern breakfast of sausage, home fried potatoes, biscuits with brown gravy, and eggs however you wanted them – he took his over medium. In addition to coffee and orange juice, the drink table had regular milk, nonfat milk, buttermilk, grapefruit juice, cranberry juice, and apple juice. Morgan overate, but reckoned since he planned to be outside in the hot sun all day, he'd burn off any excess calories. Besides, he was taking full advantage of real breakfasts for a change, not the nearly inedible stuff his cook did in Kazbektun, or the rabbit fodder that Europeans called breakfast.

His plan was to watch the Independence Day Parade, which was set to begin at 11:45. An annual spectacle that included school marching bands from each of the fifty states, the District of Columbia, and the territories, it was something he'd always promised himself he'd see one day. Around nine, he wandered down toward Constitution Avenue, and then went east on Constitution until he reached the Department of Commerce building at Fifteenth and Constitution. A large crowd had already gathered, about ten deep from the edge of the sidewalk to the wall of the building, but with his height and bulk, he was able to muscle his way to the front.

He'd heard the streets were always crowded for the parade, and indeed, the area near the Ellipse, the circular park south of the White House, was packed with people. Construction on the Washington Metro Rail system, which had been going on since 1969, further complicated things for people wanting to view the parade. It was especially constricted at Seventh Street, where the parade started, and at Twelfth Street, both places where the subway would cross under Constitution. Construction equipment and barriers around the excavation didn't leave many places for people to stand, so most of the crowd was down near Seventh Street, just west of the Washington Monument,

Charles Ray

where the parade ended.

Even though he wasn't fond of being in crowds, Morgan had to admit to himself that it had been worth it. The color guards, from schools and police departments, kids in colorful jerseys carrying American flags and riding unicycles, military school marching bands, and floats of all kinds, from schools to factories, all parading their love of country to the delight of the thousands who thronged Constitution Avenue on both sides, Americans of all ages, colors, and genders, able to put their differences aside for a couple of hours and celebrate the freedoms that others had made possible for them.

He was particularly impressed, almost moved to tears, when a group of ten Vietnam veterans marched past, five of them in wheelchairs being pushed by the other five. Vietnam had not been a popular war, and just over two months since America's ignominious exit from that country, there was still a residue of anger, some of which had been directed at the men who were sent there to fight. But, he noticed more than one person in the crowd dabbing at tears as this rag tag group wheeled past, and the cheers and shouts were not of derision, but support.

Too bad, he thought, that we can't have July Fourth every day of the year.

When the parade had passed, and people started drifting across the street to continue their celebrations on the Mall, where there would be free concerts and other entertainment, Morgan headed back to his hotel. He was soaked through with sweat, and wanted to shower and take a nap before supper, and then he'd return to the Mall for the fireworks display, another Washington spectacle he'd always promised himself.

After showering and changing into dry clothes, he fixed himself a light lunch of tuna and crackers, and ate it sitting on the end of the bed. He capped lunch off with a cold beer, and then lay back on the bed, falling asleep almost instantly.

It was after six when he woke up. He debated fixing a quickie meal, and then decided, to hell with it; he washed his face and took a light sweater on the off chance that it would get cool on the Mall after dark, and went out in search of a café or restaurant in the vicinity. In the area between Constitution Avenue – actually, Twenty-First Street – and Washington Circle, thanks to George Washington University, there's no shortage of places to eat. Morgan picked a small bistro with four tables on the sidewalk, which he skirted, preferring to eat without having to swat insects, and had a nice meal of fish and chips with a glass of red wine. He ignored the waiter's sneer when he ignored the man's suggestion that white wine would be more appropriate with fish. He hated white wine, and refused to drink it with anything.

After finishing his meal, he had a second glass of wine, and when that was finished, he called for the check. He gave the snotty little waiter a ten percent tip despite his officious nature and scornful looks, just to show he was the better man. It made him feel good to see the look of surprise on the little turd's face.

The temperature had dropped; instead of being steamy hot, it was merely warm. He tied his sweater around his waist and started for the Mall.

It was still light even at half past eight, but the Mall was already crowded, with people on the steps of the Lincoln Memorial, sitting along the edge of the Reflecting Pool dangling their feet in the water, and scattered about the grassy areas, some on blankets, some on the grass.

Morgan walked to the eastern end of the Reflecting Pool, and found a relatively under-populated stretch of grass. He spread his sweater on the grass and sat on it.

"That's a terrible way to treat such a beautiful sweater," a husky voice to his left rear said.

He turned to see a tall woman with medium

brown skin and dark brown hair with streaks of gray, spreading a blanket on the grass. She was smiling at him. He returned the smile.

"I know," he said. "But, the grass is apt to get a bit moist when it gets dark, and I don't like having a wet behind."

She laughed; a deep throaty laugh. Morgan liked the sound. "Shoot, that ain't gonna help you. You're still gonna have a wet behind, but you'll also have a ruined sweater."

He realized that she was right. He stood and picked up his sweater, shaking out the grass and dirt that had clung to the fabric.

"Guess I'll just have to watch the fireworks standing up," he said.

"Well, I suppose if you're a real nice person, I could let you share my blanket. Are you a nice person?"

There was a hint of flirtation in her voice, which surprised Morgan. She was a beautiful woman, but looked to be about his age, an age at which he didn't expect women to act the coquette. But, he thought, she is damn good looking.

"I assure you, ma'am," he said. "I'm probably the second nicest person out here right now."

"Only the second nicest? Why is that?"

"Well now, you're offering to share your blanket with me so I don't ruin my sweater. I reckon that makes you the *nicest* person here, now doesn't it?"

There was that laugh again. He could get used to hearing that sound.

"My name is David, by the way; what's yours?"

"I'm Earline," she said as she scooted to the side to make room for him on the blanket.

Chapter Eighteen

Saturday, July 5, 1975, Arlington, Virginia

After pulling night duty filling in for an agent on the secretary of state's security detail at an Independence Day reception, Diplomatic Security Special Agent Lee Kennedy was in the mood for sleeping in on Saturday morning. Unfortunately for him, his daughter Rachel was on her school's softball team and they had a morning game in an Arlington park about six miles from the house they shared. Too far for her to walk, and he didn't like letting her run about Northern Virginia unchaperoned, so he dragged himself out of bed and drove her.

DC Police detective Al Murphy called him just as he was leaving the house, saying that he had some interesting information to discuss, so Kennedy gave him the address of the ball field.

Murphy showed up about twenty minutes

after Kennedy and Rachel arrived. Kennedy was sitting in the bleachers behind home plate watching his daughter's team warm up in the field, and trying to stifle the yawns that threatened to dislocate his jaw.

"Hey, Lee," Murphy said, as he walked up and joined him. "You look like death warmed over."

"Yeah, late night last night. I had to fill in for another agent who got sick. Didn't get home until after midnight. What's up?"

"Some new information came in on the Lesley Carter killing," Murphy said. "You know how finding her purse in a dumpster kept us from treating it as a mugging gone bad, right?"

"Sure, good thing the killer was nice enough or dumb enough to do that. If he hadn't we might never have learned the truth."

"Well, it gets better, bug. The killer didn't put that purse in the dumpster. He threw it into some bushes not too far from where he killed Carter. Damn thing could have lain there for months if the old lady who lives on the property hadn't seen him do it. Pissed her off, him littering her property like that, so she went out and retrieved it. But, then she decided she didn't like the style, so she walked down a few blocks and threw it in a dumpster. She's an eccentric old bird; keeps old newspapers around for months. Few days ago she was reading one that had the news about the killing in it. Made her think of the purse, so she came in and told us what happened."

"Damn, talk about dumb luck," Kennedy said. "What're the odds?"

"Long, bub, real long. She was the lucky one, though. Said she'd planned to give the litterbug a piece of her mind, but he'd disappeared by the time she got there. Good thing, too, or we might have had two victims that night. Anyway, she gave a description of the guy and when we showed her a mug shot, she confirmed it. It was the same gunsel that you shot."

"Well, I guess that closes that case."

"Yeah, you'd think that, but, it got me to thinking, so I dug into a few more cases. I think our late friend was pretty busy around that time. There was that other fellow from the State Department, Lake something or other –"

"Dudley Lakeworth," Kennedy said. "He was Alison's boss, and was up to some real hinky shit."

"Yeah, that's him. Anyway, I had the lab boys go back over everything with a fine tooth comb, and guess what; they found a single strand of hair in the victim's clothing that wasn't his, but turned out to belong to our boy, Gawan Hart."

"That certainly would seem to link the two murders."

"Oh, buddy, it just keeps getting better. You remember that senator, the guy from Alabama?"

"Senator Longroux? Yeah, he had an accident. Fell and broke his neck or something."

"Or it was made to look like it," Murphy said. "Seems the good senator had connections with Hart back before he got elected. I'm still checking on that."

"You sayin' this Hart character killed Longroux maybe? But, if he and Longroux had a relationship from before, that makes no sense."

Murphy laid a hand on Kennedy's arm. "See, pal, if you'd had a good night's sleep your brain would be working better. What if there's someone else who was pulling Hart's strings? Somebody who was worried the senator might blab to the media – he was good at doing that – and had Hart take him out before he did?"

"Shit, you're right. But, who in hell . . . wait, there *was* another guy on the Mall that day when I saw Longroux and Hart." He laid a finger alongside his nose and cocked his head. "Yeah, it was a retired American diplomat, a guy named Hitchcock. Alison pulled up some dope on him."

"Yeah, I remember her telling me about

him," Murphy said. "But, he dropped out of sight. I suppose I'd better put him back on my list of people to check into."

Kennedy looked at Murphy, a weary expression on his face. "Does it ever stop? Every time we turn over a rock, some more maggots crawl out."

"Only way it'll stop," Murphy said. "Is if we stop turning over rocks, But, heaven help this town if we do that."

Chapter Nineteen

Monday, July 7, 1975, Washington, DC

The rest of Morgan's weekend was quiet. He spent most of Sunday reading the *Washington Post*, mostly the comics and sports page, and working the crossword puzzle in the magazine insert.

He thought a lot about the woman he'd met the previous evening, Earline, a real knockout, with her coffee with a touch of cream complexion, dark brown eyes, and full lips. Slightly large in the hips, but not grotesquely so, medium sized breasts that were still firm for her age, and he was mentally kicking himself for not getting her number. If he was going to be stuck in DC for an extended period, it would be good to have someone he could kick back with from time to time.

He turned in early Sunday night. He wanted

to be completely rested for his first day in Foggy Bottom.

On Monday morning, he rose early, put on his best suit, complete with a freshly pressed power tie in red, white and blue stripes, ate breakfast in the hotel dining room, and then hiked the three blocks to the State Department in the morning heat that was already beginning to make itself felt.

Once past the guard at the employee entrance on E Street, he had to spend some time orienting himself inside the cavernous structure with its odd and even-numbered hallways, with the even numbers from the C Street side to E Street, and the odd numbers between Twenty-First and Twenty-Third Streets. It was supposed to make it easy to find an office in the building, but some of the hallways ended in walls, without clear instructions on how to find where they resumed, and there were half-hallways that defied the numbering conventions. He supposed that those who worked in the building became accustomed to it, and found their way to where they needed to go, but to him it was just mass confusion – worse even than the Pentagon with its rings and cross corridors.

He finally, though, found the office housing the Dagastan desk. He found Samuel Gosnell bent over a thick stack of papers in an office that would have made a small janitorial closet.

When Morgan's shadow fell across the papers he was reading, Gosnell looked up in surprise.

"Ah, David," he said. "I didn't expect you so early." It was three minutes past eight.

"I would have been here earlier," Morgan said. "But, I got lost twice between the lobby and here, and had to backtrack."

"Yeah, it can be confusing. Look, would you like a cup of coffee while we're waiting."

"No thanks. I had coffee with breakfast. What are we waiting for?"

"Well, ah, there's a meeting scheduled for 9:00 in personnel. I'm supposed to escort you there, and then pick you up afterwards."

Morgan's face fell. An hour with nothing to do, he thought. It would have been helpful if he'd been told in advance that he didn't have to come so early. He didn't say anything to the young desk officer, who was probably just following instructions.

"Hm," Morgan said. "Guess I'll have to find some way to kill time for an hour, eh?"

Gosnell picked up a manila folder bulging with documents. "You could try going through the read file," he said. "It'll catch you up to what's been going on since you left post. The office next door's empty, you can use that."

Morgan took the hefty stack of paper and went into the empty office. It looked like it hadn't been occupied in some time. Wiping dust from the desk surface and the chair, he put the papers down and began going through them from the bottom of the stack, knowing the older ones would be on the bottom.

Larson and his crew had been busy since Morgan's departure, with something like a dozen dispatches on the evolving situation in Dagastan. Obviously, his replacement, Montgomery Jackson-Leigh, was one of those 'it doesn't exist until we've reported it' types. Most of the reports were boring repetitions of previous reports, but Morgan detected a worrying trend – since the arrival of the Soviets in Kazbektun, the movement of foreign diplomats, primarily those of the West, had been severely restricted. They were no longer allowed to leave the capital without receiving written permission of the foreign ministry, and the ministry had not been issuing any approvals, and all meetings with Dagastani nationals – not just government officials – had to be approved by the ministry of security. There had been a few reports of minor harassment, but so far, nothing serious.

By the time Morgan had made his way to the top of the stack, he was thoroughly depressed. Things weren't going well, and he should be there on the ground with his people, not futzing around Foggy Bottom to satisfy the need of some pencil dicked bureaucrat to pass the buck.

He was in a foul mood when Gosnell stuck his head in the door. "Ready to go, Dave? It's almost nine."

He slammed the folder shut and shoved the chair back. Gosnell, seeing his scowl, took a step backwards. "Something wrong?" he asked.

Morgan took a deep breath. No sense taking it out on this poor guy, he thought.

"No, just have a lot on my mind. Let's roll."

Gosnell seemed to know where he was going, but after the second turn, Morgan was lost. Fortunately, as they stopped in front of a door not too far from one of the interior cross corridors, he noticed an elevator a few doors down. He'd at least be able to find his way to the second floor and the employee entrance lobby – he hoped.

Gosnell stopped at the door. He had a worried look on his face.

"What's wrong?" Morgan asked.

"This is where I leave you," Gosnell said. "They only want you in the meeting. If you'll have someone call when it's done, I'll come back and get you."

"I appreciate that. I don't think I'd ever find

my way out of here on my own. Next time, I'm dropping bread crumbs."

Satisfied that Morgan seemed to have relocated his sense of humor, Gosnell smiled with relief, but he wasted no time heading back up the corridor, and was soon lost to sight around a corner.

Morgan debated knocking in the door, and then decided, to hell with it. It's an office, not someone's home, and shoved it open.

He walked in to find himself in a long, narrow room, a conference room by the looks of it. A long wooden table, about six feet in, dominated the center of the room. To his right, sat five people, four men and a woman, with yellow legal pads and number two pencils in front of them. They faced a single chair in the center of the table. On the table in front of the empty chair was a legal pad and two yellow pencils. A pitcher of water with six glasses sat on a tray in the center of the table.

Five heads swiveled in his direction, but only the woman made eye contact. As he walked toward the empty seat, Morgan scanned the five. The men were looking at his sternum, steadfastly refusing to look up into his eyes. The woman, on the other hand, had her dark blue eyes locked with his. There was a look of curiosity on her round face.

Without being invited to, Morgan sat in the

empty chair, rested his forearms on the table and looked impassively across the table. He'd decided going in that he wouldn't be the first to break the silence. The woman, toying with a stray lock of her lank, blonde hair that had fallen across her forehead, had a definite smile on her face now.

Finally, the older looking man, a hawk-beaked, gaunt, professorial looking type with more gray than brown in his thinning hair that he wore slicked back severely, cleared his throat and adjusted his already perfectly positioned blue tie. "Uh, Mr. David Morgan," he said, sounding as professorial as he looked. "I'm Matthew Cullen from personnel. I want to thank you for agreeing to join us today. The gentleman to my far left is Dane Harwood from the office of your assistant secretary." He nodded toward a mousy looking; slightly overweight man in a rumpled brown suit; with flecks of dandruff in his unruly brown hair. "To his right is Sylvester Jenkins, who is from personnel." Jenkins looked to be in his late thirties. He wore a three-piece charcoal gray suit with a tie that was almost a twin of the one Morgan wore. "To my right is Gordon Deming; also from personnel." Deming was nondescript. He wore a blue pin striped suit, blue tie, and powder blue shirt. His oval face had no distinguishing features, and his expression was as bland as oatmeal without salt. "And, finally, Ms. Catherine Logan from the office of the director general." Unlike the others, who hadn't looked at or acknowledged him as they were being introduced, Logan nodded and smiled.

"I suppose I should say I'm pleased to meet you," Morgan said. "But, considering the reason for this meeting, that wouldn't be precisely truthful."

"Uh, Mr. Morgan," Cullen said. "I think perhaps you may have been misinformed. We're merely here to determine the facts behind the unfortunate death of Ambassador Robert Ellingsworth. Since you were present at the tragic incident, it's only natural that we would like to get your version of events."

"If you've read the cable I sent after the event, you should already know my version of what happened."

"Come now, Mr. Morgan. We both know that cables are often truncated versions of what happened. You might, in retelling the incident, recall some minor fact that didn't make its way into the cable, but which might of extreme value in helping us here in the department to understand it."

The man's tone was sincere, but Morgan knew that a really experienced bureaucrat could project any emotion he chose. The fact that he refused to look him in the eye marked him as a snake in Morgan's book. On the other hand, he did have a point. There was no way everything that happened could be reported; the damn cable would be so long no one would read it.

"Okay," he said. "You have a point. What do you want to know?"

Cullen's lips twitched up ever so slightly. It was the first emotion he'd shown since Morgan walked into the room.

"Thank you, Mr. Morgan," Cullen said. "Perhaps if you'd just tell us what happened as best as you can remember?"

Morgan searched his mind for a moment, trying to decide the best place to start. Then, he related the events leading up to Ellingsworth's death, leaving out any mention of his suspicion that the man might have set up the ambush in which he was killed. He still couldn't bring himself to do that. When he'd finished his story, he sat back in his chair, gazing evenly at the five people facing him.

The four men continued to look down at their legal pads; Harwood was scribbling something. Catherine Logan was looking at him, something akin to sympathy in her eyes. Finally, Cullen broke the silence.

"Let me see if I understand this," he said. "You're saying that you were worried that the ambassador might have been involved in some unsafe activity?"

"That is correct."

"You made this known to him, I suppose?"

"I did. I told him I thought his late night meetings in some dicey parts of town; especially when he didn't share the information with me or the RSO; was potentially dangerous."

"What was his reaction to that?" asked Deming.

"He basically told me to butt out," Morgan said. "He reminded me that he was the man in charge, and that it wasn't my place to tell him what to do."

"Rightly so," Harwood said. "Ellingsworth was the president's representative, not you. What made you think you had the right to criticize his actions?"

Morgan glared at the mousy little fat man, and was about to give him a verbal lashing, but Jenkins, who was still looking at his blank pad, raised his hand. "My question, Mr. Morgan," he said. "Is why you didn't do more to stop the ambassador from such ill-conceived activity?"

Morgan's expression was incredulity. One of his inquisitors chiding him for overstepping his bounds, while the other accuses him of not doing enough. He could feel the heat rising in his cheeks. He leaned forward, clenching his fists beneath the table.

"I'm afraid you have me a bit confused," he said. "Either I broke the rules to even question what he did, or I didn't do my job because I didn't keep him from doing what he did. Which is it?"

"There's no need to be combative or defensive, Mr. Morgan," Cullen said. "This isn't an adversarial hearing."

"You could have fooled me," Catherine Logan said, leaning forward and staring at Cullen. "Dane's statement was frankly accusatory, as was Gordon's question; and, Mr. Morgan, David, has a point; which should he have done, ignored the ambassador or taken a stronger line?"

"May I remind you, Miss Logan, that this is a personnel department committee, and as an employee of the DG's office, you're here as a courtesy."

"And, is Mr. Harwood from the geographic assistant secretary's office here as a courtesy as well?"

Cullen's face reddened. "Uh, that office has a vested interest in this matter. After all, it was their embassy that was involved."

"And, Mr. Morgan is a member of the Foreign Service, thus the director general also has a vested interest. And, I can assure you that she wouldn't like to see an employee's rights trampled on."

"We're not trampling on anyone's rights," he said with his nose in the air. "Mr. Morgan is here of his own free will. If he felt his rights threatened, he could have a union representative here with him."

"Was he made aware of that?" Logan copied his pose, speaking at him down the length of her nose.

"I wasn't told I'd need anything like that," Morgan said quietly but forcefully. "In fact, until I arrived in this room, I really had no idea what this meeting would be about. So, before we go any further, I have a few questions of my own if you don't mind."

"Well, really, Mr. Morgan," Cullen said. "That is highly irregular –"

"Why," Morgan countered. "If, as you said, this is not an adversarial hearing, why can't I ask a few questions to better understand what it *is* about?"

"He has a very good point," Logan said.

Cullen's face colored more deeply, and he seemed to be having trouble breathing. The other three men were more intently focused on the table surface than before.

You sorry sons of bitches, thought Morgan, *this is nothing but a kangaroo court, and I'm the*

candidate for the rope. Well, the hell with that.
"Gentlemen, lady," he said. "I think we should maybe stop this meeting right now unless you're prepared to come clean on exactly why the hell we're here." He paused, but Cullen continued to glare at Logan, ignoring him. "That's kind of what I figured. Okay, I'm out of here. When you people are ready to treat me with a little respect, contact me through the desk officer."

He rose, staring down at Cullen, silently daring the man to say something. For the first time, Cullen looked up into his eyes. His expression at first was anger, but as he held Morgan's gaze, there was a flickering of his eyes, and he caught his breath. The anger was replaced by fear; raw, naked fear; for he was looking into the eyes of a man who'd seen death, who'd looked it in the face and refused to back down. David Morgan had been in the crucible of combat in Vietnam during some of the toughest, most violent days. He knew how to get comfortable with fear. And now, he was angry. A ball of white hot molten anger had centered itself in his gut. But, unlike many people who get excited when they get angry, Morgan became calm, unnaturally calm. Time slowed down for him, and heretofore subaudible sounds were plain to his ears. He felt as if he could hear the thudding of the heartbeats of the five people sitting across the table.

Just before he turned and walked slowly

from the conference room, David Morgan did something that chilled the blood in Matthew Cullen's veins: he looked down at the man and smiled. Not an open-mouth smile, with teeth showing in gleaming rows. Not a wide smile of friendship. No, it was a slight upturn of the corner of the mouth, a sad smile, a smile of sympathy.

Chapter Twenty

Morgan found Samuel Gosnell waiting for him in the hallway just outside the conference room.

"I wasn't sure you'd be able to find a phone, so I decided to come back and wait for you," Gosnell said. "How'd it go in there?"

"Well, as lynch mobs go they were more irritating than frightening."

Gosnell laughed. "I wasn't sure, but I figured that was what this was all about. You'd think they'd have better things to do with their time than harass you. I'm sorry you had to go through this."

Morgan put a hand on his shoulder. "No reason for you to apologize. I'll get through it okay."

Feeling the solid weight of Morgan's hand on his shoulder, Gosnell nodded.

"I have no doubt you will," he said. "I feel sorry for the numb nuts who's stupid enough to come after you. Anyway, could we go back to my office? I have some new information in from Kazbektun I think you'll want to see."

Morgan could have sworn that they went back by a different route than the one they'd taken to get to the conference room. He shrugged. *No matter*, he thought wryly. *I have no intention of applying for a job in this rat hole.*

Back in Gosnell's tiny office, the desk officer handed him a small sheaf of papers, cables recently received. As he read the top one, his spirits sank. The embassy had reported that soldiers of the Dagastan army had replaced the civilian police who stood guard at the entrance to the embassy; had in fact done this at every western embassy. This served as a chilling factor on locals coming near foreign embassies; even visa applications dropped off precipitously. The second cable said that local employees of the embassy had reported receiving threats if they didn't quit working for the imperialists. Absenteeism among the local staff was high, and some embassy services had had to be curtailed.

"Looks like things are going from bad to worse," Morgan said.

"I got a call from Dennis Larson," Gosnell said. "Montgomery isn't helping things. He's a micromanager, he screams at the staff, and he keeps things from them. He says morale has gone into the toilet, and that's not helped by the shit the government's pulling."

"What's the bureau front office doing about it?"

"Gaylord Pepper, the country director, has been acting DAS since Monty left, and I haven't been able to get anything useful out of him. It's almost as if they've forgotten the embassy's out there."

Morgan shook his head. "It'll take a real crisis to get their attention. If someone gets hurt badly or killed, they'll sit up and take notice – you can always depend on the bureaucracy to build a new barn after the horses are all gone."

"I'm not going to pretend I fully understand that earthy little metaphor, but if you mean they have their heads up their asses until someone kicks them, I get your drift."

Morgan laughed. He found himself liking Gosnell. A young, eager young man who probably just wanted to serve his country in an exciting and meaningful job, but who found himself caught up in a byzantine bureaucracy where the number of clearance initials you got on an action memo is more important than the substance of the damn memo, where you're often judged by the number of hours you spend in the office instead of what you got done while you were there.

"I think I like your metaphor better than mine. A lot of people here certainly seem to have their heads in rectal defilade. Not much to do about it though. You got anything else on for me?"

"Not really. You might as well hang out at your hotel as here. I'll call you if anything comes up."

Chapter Twenty-One

Tuesday, July 8, 1975, Washington, DC

Lee Kennedy and Al Murphy met in a small bistro on H Street, not far from Farragut Square. They sat in a table in the back corner nursing cups of coffee.

"What's so urgent you had to see me this morning, and why couldn't you come to my office?" Kennedy asked.

The DC detective blew on his coffee, and then took a sip. He slowly sat the cup on the table, cupping it in his hands.

"I didn't think it was a good idea to be seen coming in to the State Department," he said. "This case is giving me the willies, frankly. Every time I turn over a rock something slimy crawls out. I tell you, Lee, right now, other than you, I don't know who in this town I can trust."

Kennedy regarded the man carefully. He'd known Al Murphy for several months now, and had come to think of him as a tough street cop, but he was clearly unsettled about something.

"Come on, Al, it can't be that bad, can it? I mean, even though you can't make an arrest, you pretty much know it was Hart who killed the two department employees, so what else could be bothering you?"

"Maybe I'm just being paranoid, but I still think there's more to this than meets the eye." He toyed with his cup. "I've been going back over all the case files; just to see if there might be something that was missed the first time around. With our current case load, there's no appetite for closed cases in the department, so I've been doing it on the QT, logging extra hours at night, but not putting in for overtime, so I don't attract attention."

"Now, that *is* paranoia, my friend. What? You think there might be someone in the police department in on this?"

"Hey, pal; this is Washington, DC, remember. In this town, everyone's up to something it seems. Until I have something solid, this is just between you and me."

Kennedy hadn't had much contact with people outside the State Department other than Murphy, and hadn't been in the area long enough to get a good sense of how things worked. Murphy, on the other hand, had been in the DC police department for a long time, and if he felt something was amiss, Kennedy was prepared to give him the benefit of the doubt.

"Okay, so it's just you and me for now – and, don't forget Alison. She has contacts within the intelligence community that might come in handy."

A worried look creased Murphy's face.

"Yeah, I guess she can be trusted too. But, that's it."

"Damn, man, you're acting like your life might be in danger."

"Don't laugh, it could be. Yours too, if what I think happened is true."

"And, just what do you think has happened?"

"Look, your two people getting killed; well, while they might have been important in your outfit, to me they're just two more citizens who got offed. But, when a U.S. Senator is killed, that, my friend, is big time."

"You're talking about Carlton Longroux? You still think his death wasn't an accident?"

Murphy took a sip of coffee. When he put the cup down, he looked at Kennedy, there was a haunted look in his eyes.

"I do, and I'll tell you why. I went back over the autopsy report. It didn't hit me at first, but then I noticed the ME pointed out some bruises on the body, and that bothered me."

"Bruises? What's so strange about that? He did fall, didn't he; from a second floor landing, and broke his neck on the marble floor? Wouldn't that account for bruises?"

"Yeah, according to the report, he was standing on a chair on the landing, changing a light bulb. The chair slipped and he took a tumble over the railing. According to the ME, death was instantaneous."

"So, what's strange about it?"

"Well, he had a lateral bruise across the small of his back, and that could be accounted for by the fact that he fell backwards off the chair and struck the railing on the way down. But, there were some small bruises on the inside of both arms, near the elbow. The ME noted them, but didn't think they were of particular interest. He was found by his houseman who'd been out shopping. His alibi checked out, so it was put down to an accidental fall."

"Makes sense to me."

"Yeah, and if it wasn't for all the other strange shit that's been going down surrounding this case, I'd think that too. But, hear me out on this. What if someone helped Longroux over that railing? What if someone grabbed him by the arm; shoved him against the railing, and then tossed him over? That would explain the bruise on his back. And, it's consistent with the bruises on his arm."

Kennedy considered what Murphy had just said. Damn it, he thought, now he's making me paranoid. It could have happened that way. But, there was one flaw in his argument. Who would have wanted the senator dead?

"Our late friend Hart was busy putting people away, but he'd have to have been Superman to kill Alison's boss *and* do the senator. Besides, shoving someone over a railing doesn't seem his style."

"I know, and that's what worries me," Murphy said. "That means there's another killer out there."

Chapter Twenty-Two

Wednesday, July 9, 1975, Washington, DC

The three-story red brick house, built at the turn of the century when some in Washington, DC had more money than taste, sat on a little hill, back from the street, and surrounded by a ten-foot-high brick wall. A narrow gate set in the wall opened onto a set of flagstone steps that led upward from the uneven, cracked sidewalk. There was no brass plate with a name or number beside the gate, as it was with many of the other equally ugly dwellings in the neighborhood, as if this house wanted to set itself apart from the others, looking down its nose at even those that towered over it.

Inside the wall, in addition to the house, there was a four-car garage that had been built in a later era from its semi-modern look of faux wood sliding doors and metal siding, a carriage house and servant's quarters that were built when the house was constructed, and harkened back to an era when the wealthy of the District of Columbia had live-in servants.

Of the houses on this block, though, only this nondescript dwelling still in fact had live-in domestic help. More accurately, *one* live-in domestic; a white-haired octogenarian whose smooth chocolate colored face belied his years, who had worked as butler/yardman/house manager of this place since his early forties, having taken the position when his father, who had had it before him, and had inherited it from *his* father, died. As far as he could remember, a male member of his family had worked in this place from the first day it opened.

He was paid well, hardly ever had to deal with his employer; in fact, didn't even know his name; and usually had the place to himself. This gave him time to read; his favorite pastime after watching quiz shows on the little black and white television set in his bedroom; because the duties were light. A little sweeping and dusting four or five times a week, and fixing and serving coffee once a month when all the old white men had their meeting, and of course, cleaning their foul-smelling cigar butts and ashes from the ash trays afterwards, and cleaning the brandy snifters. It wasn't unpleasant work.

So, he was put out by the old white man who always seemed to be in charge when their group met, when he showed up for the second time in the month, not with the group, but with the pudgy white man with the plastered down gray hair and the smarmy look. The last time, it had just been the two of them. This time, though, there was a third man. White, from the straightness and fineness of his jet black hair, but with a swarthy, sun-darkened complexion, a broad forehead, and high cheekbones, like that Indian on the nickel. He had a look about him, though, that especially drew the old man's attention. His eyes were like a snakes; cold and unblinking as if focusing on an unwary mouse. His lips, thick and dry looking, were turned down in a perpetual scowl. But, it was the eyes that sent icy fingers racing up and down the old man's spine.

That one is a stone cold killer, the old man thought, as the three men disappeared behind the door into the room where the old white men held their meetings.

When they'd entered the room, Senator Jonathan Appleby turned on Niles Hitchcock. His face was red, and a vein in his temple throbbed visibly.

"Goddammit, Niles, what's the meaning of this, summoning me here in the middle of the morning like this? You know we never come here during the day," he said. His voice shook with emotion. He wanted nothing more than to throttle the man who stood before him, a smug smile on his face.

Hitchcock held up a hand, palm out.

"Take it easy, my friend. You need to watch your blood pressure, you know. I just wanted to know if you'd given my proposal to come out of exile any serious thought."

"You didn't have to ask for a meeting to learn that. The answer is, yes I have, and I think you should go back to Costa Rica. The heat's still not completely off, and with the recent Soviet move into Dagastan, I fear people might start looking at your activities again."

"Surely the Committee could take care of that," Hitchcock said. "After all, what's the use of being part of such a high-powered group if you can't take advantage of it?"

Appleby took a deep breath, trying to keep his composure.

"That is not what the Committee is for, Niles, and you know it full well. We were organized decades ago to bring some bipartisan, no, nonpartisan, sanity to our national policy. We mostly keep watch on things; making a discrete suggestion here, urging a specific appointment there; just to keep the national interest uppermost in decision making as much as possible."

"That's part of your problem, Jonathan. You naively believe that people are capable of such magnanimity. Politics, contrary to what many say, is *not* the art of compromise; it's the *act* of governing."

"But, we govern with the consent of the people, Niles," Appleby said. "That's one thing you and Carlton seem to have forgotten. God rest his soul, Carlton just never got it."

"Oh, I think you got him all wrong," Hitchcock said. "He might have been a pompous blowhard who loved the limelight and the sound of his own voice too much, but when push came to shove, he thought a lot like you. This nonsense about the people having the final say; and, that's what it is, nonsense. Only the fit should make the decisions, and the average person is just not fit. Carlton didn't get that."

"And, just who decides who's fit and who's not? You, I take it, consider yourself one of the fit."

Hitchcock laughed, harsh and guttural. "You're damned right I am."

"You know, when I convinced the Committee to admit you, I thought it a good idea. We needed some fresh blood, and I thought you and your group, with your experience in international affairs, would bring that. I think I was wrong."

"No, Jonathan, you were right. The Committee does need fresh blood and a new outlook. You people have become too comfortable in your positions, too afraid to do what's necessary to ensure American regains and retains its world dominance."

"You sure you don't mean domination, Niles?"

"What's the difference? You people are sitting idly by and allowing our position in the world to erode. That has to stop, and the Committee, under the right leadership, could be the mechanism to stop our decline."

Appleby shook his head, causing his mane of white hair to wave in the air.

"No, no, you just don't understand," he said. "Firstly, we've never been about American domination. America must learn to live as part of a diverse world. Yes, we have the greatest economic and military power, but we must learn to use that power wisely. The polarization of partisan politics tends to obscure that. We seek to moderate partisan impacts."

"Oh crap," Hitchcock said. "Don't tell me you old farts are part of the smaller government crowd; that bunch that wants to totally emasculate the government?"

"Of course not. We believe that government should be as large as it needs to be to satisfy the will of the people. The belief that the best government is that which governs least is fallacious. The best government is simply that which governs best, and in a democracy, that means giving the people what they need."

"Hmph. That works only when the people know what they need."

"You don't think the American people are smart enough, given the right information, to make informed, intelligent choices?"

"Some are, but you must admit that the vast majority are not, and never have been. Even at the founding, the framers of our Constitution had their doubts about giving the vote to everyone. Wasn't it John Adams who said that men without money or property shouldn't have the same voice in government that men with property have? He, and many like him, feared universal suffrage because they felt it could lead to class revolution. Well, look around you, Jonathan. You have the blacks clamoring for a bigger share of the American pie, women pushing for abortion rights; one group after another seeking to dilute our power. We can't take away the right to vote, but we can ensure that the right people are in the positions that count."

"That is such a cynical attitude. I can't believe that all of your fellow Foreign Service Officers think like you."

"Hah! Of course they don't. But it really doesn't matter. We have the White Dragons, a small, tightly-knit of officers who know what's important. The rest, like the vast majority of the public, don't really count. They're just supporting players to ensure that we're available to those in power when we're needed."

"Heaven help us if too many like you ever come to power. Thank goodness we had men like Patrick Henry and George Mason among the founding fathers, men who truly believed in government for the people, of the people, and by the people."

"Oh, every generation has had to deal with people like that; those too soft to take the actions necessary to truly prosper. But, the tide of history has fortunately swept them aside."

"Seems to me, it's more your crowd that gets swept aside. The people are still the ultimate bosses in this country."

Hitchcock's face colored, and his eyes blazed.

"That may be," he said. "But, right now, my concern is with the leadership of the Committee."

Appleby's expression was hard. "If, Niles, you're suggesting that *you* are the one to chair the Committee, let me assure you that will never happen. The others would never accept it."

"They would if you were to name me."

"And, why would I do that?"

Hitchcock turned and inclined his head toward the other man, who had remained as motionless as a wooden statue throughout their conversation, the only movement, his eyes that constantly scanned the room in front of him.

"Jonathan, permit me to introduce my new associate, Mr. Ignacio Batista. Mr. Batista is a specialist; you might say a pest control specialist of sorts."

"*Con mucho gusto, senor,*" Batista said, inclining his head slightly.

"Please to meet you, Mr. Batista," Appleby said; then his eyes went wide. "Wha-, what do you mean pest control?"

"He gets rid of things that bother me," Hitchcock said, laughing harshly. "And, he quite enjoys his work."

"Are you threatening me?"

"My, my, now you're beginning to sound like Carlton. You should know by now, Jonathan, I don't threaten. Let's just say I'm giving you something to consider. Come Ignacio, let's take our leave. Senor Appleby has a lot to think over."

He turned on his heel and strode toward the door. Batista, with one last look at Appleby as if he was a fly about to be swatted, turned and followed. The sound of the door closing was hollow, reverberating inside Appleby's skull. Even though it was one of the hottest days of the hottest months of the year, he felt a chill.

Outside in the hallway, Hitchcock and Batista marched toward the exit, Hitchcock with a satisfied smile on his face, Batista impassive.

Neither of them noticed the elderly black man standing in the hallway just outside the door dusting a suit of armor. To them, he was no more than another piece of furniture, something that came with the house, and thus of no concern. They didn't even look his way as they passed within three feet of him, nor did they acknowledge his presence. He didn't turn as they passed, so they also didn't see the way his eyes narrowed and his lips curled down at the ends.

Chapter Twenty-Three

Thursday, July 10, 1975, Washington, DC

Three days of sitting around his room, or walking the Mall – including visits to the museums in the Smithsonian complex at the east end of the Mall – had done little to improve Morgan's mood. It had instead given him too much time to brood over the way he'd been treated at the 'meeting.'

He woke early on Thursday determined to force the issue one way or another.

Around nine, he walked down to Foggy Bottom. With a bit of trial and error, and by doubling back a couple of times, he managed to find Samuel Gosnell's office without having to ask directions.

"Morning, Dave," Gosnell said. "What're your plans for this morning?"

Morgan was beginning to really like the desk officer, even if he did ask the most inane questions.

"Nothing really; just thought I'd check and see if there was anything new in from post, or maybe some new scuttlebutt about what the executioners in personnel have planned for me."

Gosnell laughed. He wasn't sure if the latter comment was meant to be funny, but the look on Morgan's face as he uttered it made him feel comfortable laughing.

"Nothing new from post, just more of the same. Monty keeps pissing everyone off and putting his foot wrong. As to your situation here in the building, no one's talking to me about it. There was a request from INR, though. Alison Chambers, an analyst, has been working this from the beginning, and she'd like to talk to you first hand to get your impressions."

Morgan's face fell. "If I remember correctly, INR is on the top floor, at the end of some really twisty hallways, and behind steel doors. Am I expected to find my way there on my own?"

"No, I'll take you. I don't know how long you'll be there, though, and I have a meeting out of the building in an hour, so I might not be able to pick you up and show you how to get out."

"That's okay," Morgan said. "I'll get Ms.

Chambers to show me. I've spoken to her on the phone, and she seems like a straight up person."

"Yeah, for a civil servant, she's not bad."

The journey from Gosnell's office to the main entrance door of the Bureau of Intelligence and Research, known in the building simply as INR, was as confusing as Morgan had feared. Even with a written map, he'd have been hard-pressed to find the place, tucked as it was in a dog leg of a dark corridor.

Gosnell pushed a button beside a large steel door. A tinny voice asked their business, and he informed the disembodied voice that he was delivering David Morgan to see Alison Chambers. The voice mumbled something unintelligible, and there was a loud click. Gosnell heaved the door outward.

"Here you go," he said. "Alison's office, if I remember, is the second on the left, just before you get to the secretary's desk. Don't ask me why they don't have the secretary in the front. This is INR, and when you deal with them, you learn not to ask too many questions."

As the heavy door closed behind him with a sighing noise, Morgan took stock of his surroundings. He was in a moderately wide hallway, with two doors on each side. It opened up into what looked like a wider area with a large wooden desk sitting squarely in front of the hallway, so that if you had to go somewhere other than the first four offices, you had to pass the secretary. Morgan could see no one at the desk. He walked to the second door on the left, which was ajar, and stuck his head in. A young woman with mussed brown hair, wearing a blue blouse and gray skirt that displayed a rather nice pair of legs, sat at a desk hunched over a map and a scattering of papers.

"Excuse me," Morgan said. "Are you Alison Chambers?"

She jumped up as if she'd been goosed.

"Oh, my goodness," she said. "I didn't even hear you come up. Yes, I'm Alison . . . you must be David Morgan . . . please come in and have a seat."

She hurriedly swept another untidy pile of papers off the only other chair in the room, causing them to drift lazily to the floor where they landed in an untidy scattering.

"Sorry for the mess," she said. "I've been trying to educate myself to Dagastan. Strange little place."

Morgan extended his hand. Her grip was strong. "Yes, I'm David Morgan," he said. "You can just call me Dave." He sat. "If you think Dagastan's strange looking at it from here, you should try living there. Strange hardly captures the place."

"That's precisely why I wanted to talk to you," she said. "To get your view of what it's like on the ground. It'll really help me do a better analysis."

"Anything in particular you want to know?"

"I want to know everything, so why don't you just tell me what you think is important for me to know."

So, he told her about Dagastan; it's history, current events, the goings on at the embassy under the late ambassador, and the arrival of Soviet forces. She took notes, writing furiously on a steno pad as he talked, stopping him occasionally to ask for a clarification, or the spelling of a name.

They'd been at it for almost two hours when the sound of a throat clearing yanked them out of the academic reverie into which they'd fallen.

"Ahem, excuse me, Alison, but . . ."

As Morgan turned, the breath caught in his throat. Standing in the doorway, her mouth open, was the beautiful, brown goddess he'd spent an enchanted evening with. She seemed as surprised to see him as he was to see her.

"Well, hello there," he said, standing and putting out his hand. "Fancy meeting you here. You didn't tell me you worked for the State Department."

"You never asked me where I worked," Earline Brown said. "In fact, you never even asked my name."

She took his proffered hand. Her skin felt warm and smooth in his hand.

"True, and I kicked myself for the rest of the weekend for that stupid oversight. Let's start over. Hello, I'm David Morgan."

"Uh, I . . . I'm Earline Brown. Pleased to meet you . . . again."

A confused looking Alison Chambers stood. "I'd introduce you two, but it seems that you already know each other – sort of. How did you two meet?"

"We shared a blanket together Saturday night," Morgan said.

"Hey," Brown said. "What he means is, I let him sit on my blanket to watch the fireworks on the Mall so he wouldn't ruin a perfectly good sweater."

Her brown cheeks became darker with a reddish undertone, and her eyes blazed at Morgan.

"Right," he said. "That's what I meant."

She made an 'hmph!' sound. "You didn't tell me that you worked for the department either."

Looking down, she realized that she was still

holding his hand. She snatched her hand back quickly, blushing.

"I apologize for that," he said. "I guess the beauty of the fireworks . . . and, other things, sort of distracted me. I hope you'll let me make up for it."

"And, how do you propose doing that?"

"Well, I was thinking I could take you to lunch or dinner, or even lunch *and* dinner, for starters."

Chambers, who had been ignored by both, looked from one to the other like a spectator at a ping pong match, a bemused look on her face.

"Hel-l-lo, children in the house," she said. "I'm still here, guys." She turned to Brown. "You wanted to see me about something, Earline?"

"Uh, oh . . . oh, yeah," Brown said. "I was thinking about knocking off a little early for lunch and heading up toward the White House. One of those restaurants on G Street near Pennsylvania Avenue with the tables outdoors, and I was wondering if you wanted to come."

Even though she spoke to Chambers, her eyes never left Morgan's face.

"That sounds like a great idea," Morgan said. "Why don't you let me treat you both?"

"I like it," Chambers said. "Can we leave in a

few minutes; I still have a few more questions I need to ask Dave."

Brown shot her a glare, a look that she missed. But, Morgan caught its twin which she zinged his way, a brief flicker of annoyance at him. At first, he was perplexed, and then his heart did a flip flop – she was upset that he'd included Alison in the invitation. *Want me all to yourself, do you? Well, that can be arranged.*

"So," he said. "That's lunch today, and dinner tonight, right?"

The frown on Brown's face quickly transformed into a smile, and her cheeks darkened again.

Morgan gave himself a quick pat on the back. Still able to react to a developing situation and turn it to good advantage was his thought. It had served him well on combat patrols in Vietnam, had kept his career more or less on track since becoming a diplomat – the current imbroglio notwithstanding, and it was far from over yet – and, it would help him get close to Earline Brown.

"That sounds nice," she said. "I get off work around six. You want to meet me downstairs around then, or would you rather make it later, and pick me up at my house?"

"I didn't rent a car, but I suppose I could get a cab. It's your call."

"Hm, you can take me home in a cab after dinner. Let's just meet downstairs at six."

Chambers stood, grabbing her purse from the drawer, completely oblivious to the interchange playing out between Morgan and Brown.

"Okay, I can ask my questions later. Right now, I'm starved. Let's go get some lunch."

Chapter Twenty-Four

Friday, July 11, 1975, Capitol Hill, Washington, DC

Lunch with Chambers and Brown had been fun. The two women were good friends and were comfortable in each other's company. Morgan liked them both, albeit in very different ways, and fit right in, making a companionable threesome.

He'd met Brown just after six at the E Street entrance to the building, and the two of them had walked arm in arm to a restaurant on Seventeenth Street near Farragut Square. A bottle of wine had loosened both of them up, so that by midnight, when by mutual agreement they decided the evening should end, and he put her in a taxi, they had shared life histories, and she'd convinced him to agree to go on a picnic in East Potomac Park on Saturday.

He slept late on Friday, being pulled out of sleep around eight by the clanging of the phone on the table at his bedside.

"Hello," he said in a sleepy voice.

"Mr. Morgan, sorry if I woke you," a gruff voice said. "I'm Senator Jonathan Appleby, and I believe it would benefit both of us if we met."

"Huh, uh, Senator . . . well, sure," Morgan said. His head was beginning to clear. Too much wine, he thought. Got to watch that. "Isn't this a little irregular, though? I mean, meetings with members of congress are usually arranged through the Bureau of Legislative Affairs."

"I'm sure L would like to think that's the case; or at least convince all you FSOs that it is," Appleby said. "The truth is, in this town things work because individuals take the action necessary to make them work, not because of some bureaucratic organization that more often than not ends up gumming up the works. Do you think you could be in my office by ten?" He gave Morgan the room number and building in the Senate office complex.

"Yes sir, I can be there. You mind telling me what this is all about?"

"I will when you get here, son. Some things are best not discussed over an open phone line." And, he broke the connection.

Morgan rolled out of bed, showered hastily, and dressed in his best suit. He went downstairs and grabbed a piece of toast and a paper cup of coffee and walked outside eating it. Luckily, he was able to get a cab quickly, and he asked to be taken to the corner of Constitution Avenue and First Street, near the main entrance to the Russell Senate Office Building.

Going inside, he showed his diplomatic passport, and after a cursory scan with a metal detector, the guard waved him through. He checked the directory for Appleby's office, and decided to take the stairs.

The senator's office was in a wide, marble-floored hallway, with doors on each side, and in front of each door was a large state flag of the occupant's state. The hallway was empty except for him, and the only sound was the hollow echo of his footsteps. He pushed open the double doors beside the flag of North Dakota and entered the reception area.

There was no one at the reception desk. He looked around. Except for a large set of double doors to the left of the desk which were slightly ajar, the other three doors were closed. The place was as silent as a graveyard at midnight. His first instinct was to turn and leave, but on a hunch, he walked to the double doors and peeked inside.

Jonathan Appleby was sitting behind a large wooden desk, idly spinning a globe that sat in the center. The desk was otherwise bare. At the creak of the doors opening, he glanced up, a smile creasing his ruddy face.

"You must be David Morgan," he said. "You're prompt. I like that. Please come in and have a seat. I'd offer you some coffee, but since we're on recess, I decided to let my staff take some much needed vacation, and I haven't figured out how to make a decent pot of coffee. I can offer you a soft drink, though."

Morgan crossed the floor and extended his hand. The senator took it. His grip was firm and dry. Morgan could feel calluses on the man's palm.

"That's okay, sir," he said. "I had coffee just before coming."

Appleby motioned toward the large, high-backed chair in front of his desk.

"Well, why don't you make yourself comfortable, and we can talk."

When Morgan was settled, Appleby leaned forward, resting his elbows on the desk, and cupping the globe in his hands.

"Now," he said, fixing Morgan with a steady gaze. "You're probably wondering why I asked you to come here."

"Well, senator, I figure you'll tell me in your own good time."

Appleby chuckled. "I like your style, son. You mind if I call you David?"

"Most people just call me Dave, sir," Morgan said. He wasn't about to ask if he could call the senator Jonathan.

"Okay, Dave it is then. Before I get to the guts of why I asked you here, let me give you a little background. I've been in politics for a good bit of my adult life. I entered politics in the first place because I wanted to make a difference, to make our country better. Sadly, with each passing year, there are fewer and fewer of us here in congress that feel that way. Nowadays, it's all about getting votes; getting re-elected. The national interest hardly gets considered." His face looked sad as he talked. "It's getting to be the same with the bureaucrats as well. Most of 'em are just trying to hang onto their jobs until retirement; doing just enough to get by and no more."

Morgan had no firsthand knowledge of politicians other than the occasional congressional delegation he'd encountered during his assignments abroad, but he could definitely agree with the decline in the bureaucracy.

"Why do you think it's like that, senator?"

"I wish I knew. It seems to me that we go through these crises from time to time when human nature raises its ugly head. Hell fire, the bricks in the ancient city of Babylon had stories of corrupt artisans and city officials carved into them. Sometimes it's been worse than others, like our Teapot Dome Scandal, or the way the railroads cheated people and the government. Every political party's been involved, and hardly a state, major city, or even the federal government's been spared. Look at Watergate. I mean, the president himself involved up to his beady eyes."

"Damn, sir, you make it sound like everyone's crooked. What kind of hope is there for the country in a situation like that?"

"Yeah, I know I come across as a bit alarmist sometimes," Appleby said, and chuckled. "Guess that's the politician in me – always got to orate. It gets' your attention, though, don't it. Not everyone's crooked. I work with a few of my colleagues and others, from both parties, to sort of keep an eye on things, and try to keep them from swinging too far. Problem is, like I said, it's not just the politicians. I used to think you Foreign Service guys, being away from Washington so much, were immune to the infection, but lately I've learned that even you folks have a few who put other interests before the country."

"Well, like you said, it's human nature,"

Morgan said. "I was in the army, and in Vietnam, I knew officers who put their careers before the safety of their men or the mission. I reckon people have always been like that; all the way back to Babylon apparently; but, we're supposed to have institutions to catch the bad ones."

"We do, son, and they do catch 'em, but sometimes not before they've already caused great harm. Be nice if we could prevent it."

Morgan shrugged. Sure, he thought, it would be nice, but that's not the way the world works. Sometimes, despite the best you can do, bad things will happen.

"Now," Appleby continued. "That brings us to your situation. I understand they've put together some kind of kangaroo court to try and pin what's happening in Dagastan on you."

While he thought he should be surprised that Appleby knew what was happening to him, he found that he was not. The longer he stayed in Washington, the less surprised he was at the weird things that happened there.

"I, uh, suppose you could call it that," he said.

Appleby regarded him through narrowed eyes. "You weren't responsible for that fool Ellingsworth's death, were you?"

"No. Senator. I. Was. Not."

"Didn't think so," Appleby said, leaning back in his chair. "Just had to hear it from you is all. I think our friend died from the complications of overreach, a disease that seems to affect a lot of people in this town. You know, his secretary is the one who got this started, alleging that you set it up."

"I have two other people in the embassy who can prove that the meeting where he was killed was the ambassador's idea. He picked the time and place."

"And, he'd been having these little clandestine meetings for some time, right, but it just happened that *this* meeting, the first you'd been invited to, was ambushed. Doesn't that strike you as odd?"

Morgan felt his chest tighten. He wanted to share his suspicions with someone, but he wasn't sure he could trust this elderly politician who seemed to know more about what was going on than some of the people at the center of events. In fact, Morgan was beginning to wonder if Appleby wasn't sitting at the center of things, like some giant spider sitting in the center of its web, alert to vibrations on the far perimeter signaling fresh prey.

"Yes, sir, I guess you could say it was strange," he said. "But, I don't have any proof of how it came about."

Appleby's head moved up and down slowly.

"Of course, move with caution. Rash thoughts and rash actions have led more than one person to his downfall." He clapped his hands and leaned forward. "Well, what we've got to do is settle this mess with you. You just be patient. I'll make a few phone calls. It'll take a few days, but I think your troubles should go away soon."

"You can do that, senator?"

"One of the prerogatives of the position. I'm not without a modicum of influence. One more thing, son. One day I might be calling on you, and I would hope you'd answer."

There it was, Morgan thought. There's seldom a *quid* without a *quo*. He stiffened. Appleby raised his hands and waved them from side to side.

"No, son," Appleby said. "It's not what you think. I'm doing what I'm doing for you because it's the right thing to do. I think you have potential, and you strike me as someone who puts your country first. I would hope that should the chance to do that present itself in the future, you'd be ready."

"I took an oath to serve the country," Morgan said. "As long as I'm employed by the government, I'll honor that oath." He wasn't totally convinced of the politician's sincerity, but the man certainly seemed sincere. For now, he thought, if he could make the problem with personnel go away, Morgan was willing to play along.

Chapter Twenty-Five

Morgan took a taxi back to Foggy Bottom, entering the building through the ceremonial entrance on C Street. Even though he had no desire to work in the place, he had to admit to being impressed by the towering glass wall with the flags of all nations that ran across the back of the lobby, and the somber tone struck by the grayish marble plaques listing the names of American Foreign Service Officers who had died in the line of duty. The barrel had a few soft apples in it, but it was still a barrel he was proud to be in.

He went to Gosnell's office and asked for directions to diplomatic security. He wanted to talk to someone about the worsening situation in Dagastan. Gosnell told him how to get to the one agent he knew, Lee Kennedy. Kennedy had briefed Gosnell when he started work, and the desk officer had learned that Kennedy had been involved in the investigation of the murder of his predecessor.

On an upper floor like INR, diplomatic security wasn't quite so hard to find. Morgan pressed the buzzer beside a plain wooden door, and was rewarded with a click instead of a voice asking him his business. He entered a long hallway with doors on both sides similar to INR, but the receptionist here was at the front. Morgan identified himself and asked to see Lee Kennedy. The young man on duty at the reception desk pointed down the hall.

Morgan found the agent sitting at his desk, sipping coffee from a cracked mug and reading the sports section of the *Washington Post*. He was the first person Morgan had encountered who wasn't poring over some official document or talking into the phone.

"You Lee Kennedy?" he asked.

Kennedy carefully folded the newspaper and shoved it aside. "That's me, what can I do for you?"

Morgan introduced himself and explained his reason for being there.

Kennedy shook his hand vigorously. "So, you're the infamous David Morgan," he said, smiling broadly. "Alison said she spoke to you yesterday. Sit, sit."

When Morgan was seated in the chair next

to the desk, he leaned forward.

"I'm not sure you can help me," he said. "But, I've been following things in Kazbektun, and they seem to be getting worse. I'm not sure the guy they sent to replace me is clear on how to ask for help if it hits the fan. Worse, I'm not sure there's a damn thing I can do from here, but I have to try."

Kennedy sat back frowning.

"I know how you feel, Dave. Fact is, your instincts are right on all counts. From what Pete Jeffers tells me when he calls, this guy Jackson-Leigh can't find his ass with both hands, and he doesn't listen to the people who know what the hell's happening. Unfortunately, it really doesn't matter, because there's not a damn thing we can do if the place blows up anyway."

"Wha-, what the hell do you mean by that?" Morgan asked.

Kennedy splayed his hands out on the desk, pressing so tightly the skin around his knuckles whitened.

"A lot of people don't know this," he said. "Because it's never publicized, but, there are a few places in the world where unless we're prepared to start World War III, our embassies are hung out to dry if things go bad."

"Hung out to dry? As in, there wouldn't be

an evacuation?"

"Just so. Think about it; in order to pull Americans out of Dagastan, our forces would have to penetrate Soviet territory. Last time I checked, Ivan wasn't giving our military overflight rights, so it would mean going in without permission, which is an act of war. Besides, the thinking among the bureaucrats here in DC, when it comes to Dagastan at least, is there aren't a large enough number of American citizens there to warrant it. I mean, mainly you have the embassy folks."

"And, they're expendable," Morgan said.

"Ours not to reason why," Kennedy said.

"Ours but to bitch and cry, just before we die," Morgan finished for him. "Damn, you'd think they'd let people going there know that."

"You think so?" Kennedy said. His brows shot up. "And, how many people do you think would agree to being assigned there?"

"Maybe people with families, but we don't have any there now. Our people are either single or they left their families here in the states so the kids would have access to schools. I think you might be surprised at how many people who'd go."

"Yeah, maybe you're right," Kennedy said. "But, we'll never know, because the big cheeses in the building are never gonna risk it."

"It just seems like a shitty way to treat people," Morgan said.

Kennedy laughed harshly.

"And, the shit just keeps on flowing downhill, don't it."

Chapter Twenty-Six

Earline Brown had agreed to meet Morgan for dinner at a seafood restaurant just off Maine Avenue in the Waterfront area. When Morgan got out of the cab, he had second thoughts; the area was a little seedy, and the restaurants, on the edge of the Washington Channel, though brightly lit inside, were surrounded by dimly lit parking lots.

She was waiting for him just inside the door to the large, cavernous eating establishment whose water side was a set of large plate glass windows giving a panoramic view of the channel, East Potomac Park, and beyond the park, the Potomac River. She wore a light blue blouse that, with the top two buttons undone, showed an amazing expanse of cleavage, and a darker blue skirt that stopped just before her knees. She'd had her hair done, with a tress curled across her forehead. A hint of purple eye shadow set off her eyes.

Morgan took her hand and kissed it lightly.

"You, my dear, look absolutely ravishing," he said.

"My, aren't you the gentleman," she said, blushing.

A short, pudgy kid with sandy hair and freckles all over his face, wearing a white apron over a horizontally striped shirt that made him look fatter, came over and asked if they had a reservation. Morgan looked around the place – it wasn't crowded. He informed the kid that they didn't. Formalities satisfied, the kid took them to a table for four with a view out the window, left two menus and disappeared.

Almost immediately, a short blonde with broad hips, thick legs and a flat chest came to take their orders. Remembering the headache he had after a bottle of wine shared with Earline during their first dinner date, Morgan ordered a draft beer, while she ordered a glass of white wine. They both ordered the special, a combination of fried grouper, crab cakes, and two kinds of shrimp, with potato salad and cheese biscuits. Their drinks were brought to the table right away. The waitress said their food would take twenty to thirty minutes.

When she'd gone, Morgan lifted his beer.

"Here's to the most beautiful woman in the

place," he said.

"Aren't you the sweet one," Brown said, as she clinked her wine glass against his mug. "You know just the thing to make a woman feel special."

He took a long drink, and wiped the foam from his lips.

"Just telling the truth."

She looked at him over the rim of the glass. There was a smoldering look in her eyes. The dance was about to begin; the two-step as they circled slowly around each other, each sizing the other up; him tap dancing around his true intentions, not wanting to be too forward and making an outright pass at her, but at the same time, making his ultimate intentions clear – of course, he wasn't actually sure just *what* his actual intentions were at that moment. He enjoyed her company immensely, and found himself physically attracted to her, but having been a bachelor for so long, he didn't want to do anything that might imply a long-term commitment. Her look, as she played the coquette, said that she too was interested, but he couldn't be sure she didn't have something more permanent in mind.

"Tell me," she said. "How come a handsome man like you hasn't been snatched up?"

"I could ask you the same thing," he said.

"You're a fine looking woman – a real fine looking woman – why aren't you married?"

"Oh, I don't know. I guess I just never found the right man."

"Have you been looking in the right places?"

"Hmph! I spend ten to twelve hours a day, five days a week, locked behind a thick steel door. Not too many eligible men ever come to INR, and none of the ones who work there interest me. On Saturdays and Sundays, I'm usually too tired to leave my house. Besides, that's the only time I have to do housework. I've been out to dinner with a man exactly twice in the past year."

"Uh, you mean your two dates with me are your first in a year?"

"You sound surprised."

She was making sheep's eyes at him. That made him nervous, and excited him at the same time. There's a lot of pent-up passion here, he thought. I have to be careful not to start a fire I can't put out.

"I guess I am," he said. "I sort of figured you for a person with an active social life."

A frown crossed her face, but the waitress bringing their food short circuited whatever she intended to say. They were silent for a few minutes as they picked at their food.

He finally broke the silence, "I hope you aren't offended by what I just said."

She put her fork down.

"I'm not offended; I just don't know what you meant by that. Are you implying that I'm some kind of party girl or something?"

"Not at all. I just thought a good looking woman like you would have men standing in line to take her out."

"I told you, most of the men I meet work in the State Department. The ones that aren't too young or too old are usually so caught up in their careers, and so full of themselves, they don't have time for anyone else; or, they're married. You still didn't answer my question; why have you never married?"

Good question, he thought. One I've never given much thought to.

"Well, for a long time I was in the army. The jobs I did weren't conducive to a happy married life. Most of the guys in my units who got married, got dumped. I had one buddy who'd gone through four wives. I couldn't see doing that. It wouldn't be fair to me or to a woman. Then, I joined the Foreign Service, and I've had a string of assignments in places like Dagastan. I wouldn't want to drag a wife to places like that, and I darn sure wouldn't want to try living apart."

"You ever think that if you found the right woman, you could make it work, even in places like Dagastan. You got some couples that have stayed together in some pretty bad places."

"I suppose you're right," he said. "I haven't found that right woman yet, though."

She laughed. Her eyes flashed when she laughed.

"Why is it I think you haven't really been looking? I know men like you, David Morgan. You don't have any trouble finding willing women, and I'll bet you've had a string of them."

"Not as many as you think."

That silenced her. They turned their attention back to the food. When their plates and glasses were empty, they ordered a second round of drinks. The crowd that had been in the place when they arrived had started thinning out until half the tables were vacant. Outside the window they could see the lights on sail boats in the channel, and in the Potomac beyond, they could see the strings of lights on the dinner boat that plied the river at night.

"You know," she said. "I've always wanted to go on one of those midnight dinner-dance cruises."

"What are you doing next weekend?"

"You asking me out again?"

"Is that a yes?"

"I guess it is."

Chapter Twenty-Seven

Monday, July 14, 1975, Washington, DC

Morgan was in the State Department just before eight on Monday morning. He went first to Gosnell's office to get the location of Matthew Cullen's office.

He found Cullen in his office, on the third floor, in a corner office overlooking Twenty-Third Street and the Naval Medical Research facility. Cullen's secretary was a gaunt woman with jet black hair and an English accent. She checked to see if her boss was free. When she told him who was there to see him, he came to the door of his office, a hopeful look on his face.

"Well, Mr. Morgan, I do hope you've decided to cooperate fully with our inquiry," he said. "It would make things go so much easier."

Morgan brushed past him, ignoring his proffered hand.

"Yeah, I guess it would. Sort of like the prisoner putting the rope around his own neck."

Cullen's eyes widened.

"Why, er, no, it's not like that at all. You completely misunderstand –"

"Do I?" Morgan's eyes blazed. He clenched his fists. Cullen stepped back against the wall. "Then, tell me; why didn't you tell me about Vera Cotton's accusations? Why was I not allowed to confront her and ask for some kind of proof of what she's alleging?"

"Uh, well, it wasn't exactly that kind of meeting," Cullen said. "It wasn't adversarial, just fact-finding."

Morgan advanced on him, causing him to cower against the wall, his hands held up as if to defend his body against blows.

"Listen, Cullen, I'm tired of being jerked around. You've been dicking with me from the start, and it stops here. Either you come clean about what's up, or I'll go to AFSA and file a labor grievance."

"Now, now, there's no need for that. I'm sure we can deal with this just between us and you like civilized people. I don't see any need to involve the union in this."

"As an employee whose rights aren't exactly being respected right now, I think there's every need to involve the union. You ass holes certainly offering any kind of protection."

Cullen's face darkened. "There's no need for such vulgarity," he said.

"Friend," Morgan said. "You haven't heard vulgarity yet. I'm only mildly pissed now, but if you people keep messing with me, I will be fucking mad as hell, and trust me, you won't like me when that happens. Now, you want to tell me what evidence Cotton offered to show I was responsible for the ambassador's death?"

"Uh, well, I can't really do that."

"Can't because you're not willing to be honest, or can't because she didn't offer any?"

"It doesn't really matter," Cullen said. "I can't tell you anything."

"You're right, it doesn't matter. If you're just being a dickhead, that's bad. If you're coming after me on the basis of an unsubstantiated allegation, that's equally bad. Either way, I think it's pretty clear that I'll get nothing useful from you, so I guess my only option is to talk to the union."

"Please, don't do that," Cullen said, his face paling. "It would be better for all concerned if we could settle this without publicity. If you take it to the union, it then becomes a matter of record."

Morgan's eyes narrowed. "Are you telling me this whole thing's been handled off the radar? This kangaroo court you convened is unofficial?"

"I suppose that depends upon how you define official. As far as my office is concerned, it's official. It has no disciplinary power, if that's what you mean."

"Then, just what was it designed to do?"

"As I said at our first meeting, to ascertain the facts."

"And, just what had you planned doing with those facts?"

Cullen paled even more. He'd inched back along the wall of his office until he was wedged into the corner. His shoulders were hunched and his eyes had the expression of a trapped beast. His gaze darted from side to side.

"Uh, well, I would report them to the director of personnel, of course."

Morgan walked forward until he was less than a foot from Cullen. He could smell the man's sour breath, which held a hint of onion and stale tobacco.

"And, what would the director of personnel do with them?"

"I assure you, I don't know," Cullen said,

almost in a whisper.

"That's bullshit, and you know it," Morgan said. "You would most certainly forward your findings with some kind of recommendation; and I have a feeling you already have your recommendation prepared, and are just looking for a few facts to support it."

"B-but . . . how . . ., no, that's not so. We're still in the process of gathering the facts in this case. There's no predetermined conclusions, I assure you."

"You keep assuring me, and frankly that makes me nervous. If you're on the up and up, why the need to do that?"

Cullen had a stricken look. His lips moved, but no sound came out.

"That's what I thought," Morgan said. "Well, thanks for your time. If you have any further questions for me, send them through the union. Oh, and you might want to try using mouthwash in the morning?"

He spun and walked out of Cullen's office, brushing past the startled looking secretary who had been standing just outside the door.

Chapter Twenty-Eight

While Morgan's threat to take the issue to the American Foreign Service Association was real, he hesitated. He'd joined AFSA, which served not only as the bargaining agent for the Foreign Service, but its professional association, during his initial orientation, but except for reading the *Foreign Service Journal* every month, paying his dues, and occasionally donating to the scholarship fund, he'd had very little contact with it. His hope was that the threat, along with Appleby's promise to intervene, would be enough to make the whole thing go away.

He went back to his hotel and sat on the foot of the bed, moping and watching afternoon shows on TV.

His mind was only occasionally on the images flickering across the small screen, but when he did pay attention, he wondered why anyone would waste time; the shows were dumb. There were the quiz shows, with contestants answering stupid questions – or not – or doing something embarrassing, all the while jumping up and down like a kid on Christmas morning, while the emcee egged them on, the soap operas that stopped just short of soft porn, with a continuing cycle of infidelity, betrayal, and syrupy overacting, and entertainment shows for children. The latter were actually more entertaining that the shows for adults, but then, he figured that any adult free to watch TV in the afternoon was probably in his second childhood, unemployed, or a bored housewife just wanting to get away from dusting and cleaning.

He could, of course, have just turned the set off, but then that would have left him in the room with nothing to do, and just the sound of traffic going by on Twentieth Street. He continued to ignore the television, and just let the buzz and whistle it made keep his mind off his predicament, situation, or whatever the appropriate term was to describe his circumstances. Actually, he thought, that was probably a good word – circumstances seemed to be neutral enough on the one hand, but suitably ominous on the other.

His mind drifted to Earline Brown. A sign he needed to get back to work. Thinking about women, even a beautiful, desirable one such as

Earline, was a sign that his mind didn't have enough to occupy it. He tried to push thoughts of her out, but they pushed back.

Hell, he thought, I might as well call her. Maybe she'll want to sneak away from work and have a coffee with me, or I could walk down and have a cup of the mud the cafeteria calls coffee with her. She could say she was consulting with a colleague in Washington on consultations, which wouldn't be more than a mile or two away from the truth.

Just as he rolled over and reached for the phone, it rang. His phone stopped in midair, hovering over the handset. He looked at it as if it was a snake that had just crawled from underneath a bush.

It kept ringing.

On the fifth ring, he picked it up.

"Hello."

"Is this Mr. David Morgan?" a slightly nasal voice rang in his ear.

"Yes, who's calling?"

"Let's just say, Mr. Morgan," the voice said. "That I'm someone who has your welfare at heart, and that I wouldn't like to see anything unfortunate happen to you."

"Does a name go with that concern?"

"No names are necessary, just listen to me," the voice had clear menace in it. "Your idea of taking your problem to the union is a bad one, believe me. It could have severe consequences for all concern, you most of all."

"How the hell do you know –"

"That's not important. What's important for you to know is that I *do* know. I know all about you, Mr. Morgan, and if you're as smart as some people seem to think you are, you'll drop this matter."

"What if I decide I don't want to drop it?"

There was a long silence except for the whistling noise of a bad phone connection; then the voice came back.

"That would be truly unfortunate. One might even say it's a fatal error on your part."

"Listen you, whoever the hell you are, are you threatening me?" Morgan was beginning to get mad, boiling mad.

"Let's not be so vulgar as to call it a threat, Mr. Morgan. Let's just say it's friendly advice from someone who has your continued survival at heart. I know this is a lot for you to process, so I'll give you 24 hours to think about it. When you've slept on it, I'm sure you'll see the wisdom of my advice." The voice gave him a Washington phone number. "I'll be waiting tomorrow for your call."

The phone went dead. Suddenly, all Morgan could hear was the dull ring of the dial tone.

He put the phone back in the cradle, and sat there on the edge of the bed trying to get his mind around the conversation he'd just had – well, more of a monologue really. Who the hell was that on the phone, and how did he know so much about what was going on; things that even Morgan didn't understand. Then, it hit him. The only person who knew he was planning to take his case to the union was that bastard Cullen in personnel. It had to have been him who told the mysterious stranger about it.

Immediately, he picked the phone up and dialed the number for diplomatic security and asked to speak with Lee Kennedy.

Chapter Twenty-Nine

Tuesday, July 15, 1975, Washington, DC

Kennedy hadn't been in his office when Morgan called him the day before, but the secretary had promised to get word to him. He called Morgan at seven-thirty Tuesday morning.

"Dave, my secretary said you wanted to speak to me," Kennedy said when Morgan answered. "She said you sounded spooked."

Morgan described his phone call, including the implied threat and the instruction to call back in a day with an answer.

"Look, you'd better get over here right away," Kennedy said. "We need to talk about this."

Kennedy was waiting for him in the reception area when he pressed the buzzer, and opened the door for him.

"Come on into my office," he said.

When they were seated, Morgan leaned forward.

"Any suggestions on how to deal with this situation?"

"I've been thinking about it ever since you called," Kennedy said. "And, I have to confess, I haven't come up with anything useful. You sure you didn't recognize the voice on the phone . . . no, of course not. If you had, you'd have said so. It almost sounds, though, like someone from inside the building here."

"Or someone who has a pipeline into the building," Morgan said. "He knew about my threat to take this to the union, and the only person I told that to was that guy Cullen from personnel. It wasn't him on the phone, by the way. I would have recognized that voice of his. The guy on the phone sounded considerably older."

"Shit, pal, I'm stumped. You mind if I bring someone else in on this. The more brains working on it, the better chance of finding a solution."

"Well, I don't know." Morgan frowned. "Who did you have in mind?"

"I was thinking Alison. She's an intel analyst, and they're supposed to be good at solving puzzles."

Morgan smiled. "Oh, I don't mind if she's included. Are we going to her office?"

"Actually, I was thinking of calling and having her meet us," Kennedy said, shaking his head. "I'm starting to get paranoid about this place."

Morgan nodded. He was disappointed at missing the chance of dropping in on Earline, but Kennedy had a good point. There didn't seem to be any secrets in the building, at least not as far as his business was concerned.

Kennedy dialed Chambers' extension and asked her to meet him at the west end of the Reflecting Pool on the Mall.

"Why there?" Morgan asked. "That's right out in the open, and is likely to be crowded this time of year."

"That's the point. With so many people milling around, it'll be hard for anyone to sneak up on us without being noticeable, and eavesdropping is pretty hard with all the noise."

Morgan would have been more at home in the jungle. He'd never been involved in urban combat operations, so he trusted that the agent knew what he was doing.

The two men beat Chambers to the meeting site by a full three minutes. She was breathing hard when she came up to them.

"Did you two run here?" she asked. "I left my office as soon as I hung up. Hi, David, what's up?"

Morgan nodded at her. He didn't fail to notice the look Kennedy gave her. He smiled.

"Guess we just have longer legs, so we walk farther with each step," he said. "Thanks for coming."

"Why don't you tell Alison what you told me, Dave?" Kennedy said.

Morgan repeated his story. When he'd finished, Chambers had a stunned look on her face.

"I'd like to say I can't believe a senior official like Cullen would do something like this, but my own experience tells me it's highly likely. I wonder if Cullen is part of the White Dragons."

"You think they're involved in this?" Kennedy asked.

"They've been up to their necks in everything else," she said. "And, this sounds like their M.O."

"Does anyone know what or who the White Dragons are?" Morgan asked.

"That, my friend is the Sixty-four Dollar Question" Kennedy said. "If we knew who they were, we could probably shut them down."

"So, what do we do?"

"If I might make a suggestion," Chambers said. Both men nodded. "Dave, I think you should call this person and tell him you'll go along with his suggestion, and you won't take your case to the union. At least, not for now. Try to feel him out; see if he'll say something that might help identify him."

Morgan nodded. He didn't think it would work, but at least it would be doing something, and that beat sitting around his hotel room waiting for someone else to do something.

"Okay, I'll do that. You want me to call you tomorrow and let you know what I learned?"

"No," she said. "Call me right after you finish your call with him."

She gave him a direct line. She and Kennedy went back up Twenty-Second Street to their offices. Morgan, decided that since he was already there, he might as well enjoy the Mall, so he headed off toward the Smithsonian.

None of them noticed the swarthy man, dressed in a nondescript brown suit, standing in the trees north of the Reflecting Pool, his eyes narrowed as he watched them split up and head off in two different directions. It didn't matter, though. He hadn't been sent to follow anyone but Morgan, and Ignacio Batista was good at following orders.

Chapter 30

When Batista was convinced that Morgan was just touring the museums rather than meeting someone else, he hailed a taxi and had it take him back to the red brick house in Georgetown.

Niles Hitchcock was waiting for him in the large parlor, a large snifter of Napoleon brandy in his hand.

"Well, *mi amigo*, what do you have to report?" he asked as Batista entered the parlor.

"I followed *el negro*, the black man Morgan, as you ordered," Batista said. "He went to the, how you say, *departamento* –"

"The State Department," Hitchcock said impatiently. "So, I guess you lost track of him?"

"Only for a short while. I stood where I could

see both entrances, and after a while, he came out with the other man you tell me about, the white policeman."

"You mean, Lee Kennedy, the DS agent."

"*Si*, that is the one. The two of them went to the place of the monuments, where they were met by the woman, Senorita Chambers. They talked for a while, and then the Chambers woman and the agent went back to the . . . State Department. Morgan went to the museums."

"Did he meet anyone there, the senator you saw the other day for instance?"

"No. He walk around the museum like a *turista* for a long time. When I am sure he is not meeting anyone, I come back here."

"Could you tell what the three of them talked about?"

"No, *senor*, I could not get close enough to hear them without being seen. Is that important?"

"Yes, but I suppose that can't be helped. Well, Ignacio, my friend, I think it is regrettable that you might have to do what you specialize in very soon."

Batista smiled the smile of a hungry wolf that has smelled prey nearby.

"You wish for me to eliminate this man Morgan?"

"I fear that it will become necessary, but first, I think our friends Lee Kennedy and Alison Chambers have become too much of a nuisance."

Batista's smile widened. "You want both of them . . . removed?"

"Yes, my friend, I want you must exterminate a couple of pests. I have hope for Morgan, but we shall just have to wait and see on him."

"You want me to do the two immediately?"

Hitchcock laid a finger on his nose and closed his eyes.

"Let's wait a while, shall we. Mr. Morgan is supposed to call me later today. Let's see what he has to say. You might have an extra bit of disposal to do."

Hitchcock had never seen Batista even look at a woman, but the look that was on his face was that of erotic pleasure. The man had spent his entire adult life doing one thing, and doing it well, and now Hitchcock could see why. For Batista, killing provided the pleasure that other men found in sex. That, Hitchcock knew, could present a problem at some point, but he resolved to cross that bridge when he encountered it. At the moment, Batista was an invaluable asset.

"Just remember, Ignacio, it must either be made to look like an accident, or they must disappear off the face of the earth."

"Maybe I will do one of each," the hit man said, his eyes glistening and his chest heaving as if he was about to have an orgasm.

Hitchcock took no pleasure in killing. He much preferred having it done by someone else, but the one time he had, it had been neither pleasant nor unpleasant. Merely a task that had to be carried out and he'd done it to perfection. The police still thought it was an accident.

There was one other problem that he knew would have to be faced at some point, and he couldn't decide whether to let Batista handle it, or as he'd done before, do it himself. Jonathan Appleby was beginning to show even more signs of weakness. His drivel about the 'will of the people,' and serving the national interests made Hitchcock want to puke. He, Niles Hitchcock, had been serving the interests of the nation since graduating from college years before Appleby ever had the bright idea to run for public office. The man was, like many politicians, a chameleon, changing colors depending on his surroundings. Under certain circumstances that was a commendable trait, but at head of the Committee, he needed nerves of steel; the will and ability to do whatever was necessary to see the Committee's mission accomplished. Hitchcock knew that he had that will and ability. Like the officials who made the decision to use the atomic bomb on Japan thirty years earlier, Hitchcock knew that he was capable of doing *whatever* was necessary. If Appleby refused to step aside, and Hitchcock was afraid the man's ego would cause him to do just that, then he would have to be *pushed* aside, and in the high-stakes game they were playing, there was no golden parachute or gold watch upon retirement.

Chapter Thirty-One

Thursday, July 17, 1975, Arlington, Virginia

Lee Kennedy was leaving his house in Arlington when he saw Al Murphy's light blue Buick pull into his driveway, blocking his exit. His antenna buzzed at the sight of his cop friend outside his jurisdiction so early in the morning and the excited look on his face as he got out of the car merely added to Kennedy's unease.

"Hey, pal, you gonna invite me in for a cuppa Joe?" Murphy called as he approached Kennedy. "I had one cup of mud before I left home, and my body's screaming for another hit of caffeine right now."

"Uh . . . well, I guess I could, if you don't mind instant," Kennedy said. "But, I really need to get into my office."

"Hold your water, bub. I got some hot skinny

for you. But, I'm not talking until I got at least a half cup of coffee in me, even if it is instant. Make mine with two spoons of coffee if you don't mind."

Kennedy sighed. The man was persistent, and had some unusual ways, but he was one of the best street cops Kennedy had encountered. Clearly he had something important on his mind, and was using the jovial attitude to mask the excitement that was apparent in the glimmer in his eyes. Kennedy began to feel the stirring of excitement, like the sympathetic pains he'd felt when his ex-wife had been pregnant with Rachel.

He turned and went back inside.

"Okay, but keep it down. Rachel's still asleep."

"No I'm not, dad," her muffled voice came from behind her bedroom door. "But, keep it down anyway."

The two men laughed.

"Raising a teenager's a real ball buster, ain't it?" Murphy said. "Especially a girl."

"Tell me about it."

They went into the kitchen where Kennedy ran tap water into a kettle and put it on the stove. He then took a jar of instant coffee from the refrigerator where Rachel had insisted he keep it so it would stay fresh. He took two mugs from the counter and spooned two teaspoons of coffee into them.

"Make mine three spoons," Murphy said. "I didn't know you used these baby spoons."

Laughing, Kennedy put an extra spoon of the brown crystals into a cup. Steam was beginning to pour from the spout of the kettle. He waited until it began to make a whistling sound, and poured the boiling water into the two cups. He stirred Murphy's and handed it to him.

The cop took a sip.

"Not bad, not bad at all."

He blew on the cup, causing the vapor to stream out toward Kennedy, and then took another sip.

"Okay," he said. "Now I'm ready to talk. You better be sitting down for this."

They sat at the kitchen table. Kennedy rested his arms on the table, cradling his mug, letting the warm liquid caress his palms.

"I'm sitting, Al," he said. "Now, will you please tell me why you drove all the way out here to Arlington instead of waiting and calling me at the office?"

"Well, after I found those unexplained

bruises in the senator's autopsy report, I decided to do some digging. I called an old buddy of mine who works for the Alabama State Police," Murphy said. He leaned forward, his eyes gleaming. "First thing is he gave me the scoop on our boy, Hart. His full name is . . . was Gawan Leroy Hart, a small time gangster who operated along the Gulf Coast from New Orleans to Pensacola. Mostly extortion, but he was suspected of a string of gas station robberies and five or six unsolved murders in and around Mobile, Alabama. They were never able to get anything solid on him because witnesses either wound up missing or absent minded."

"I can believe both," Kennedy said. "The guy scared the shit out of me, that's for sure."

"Yeah, but he didn't scare you enough to keep you from putting three slugs in his chest. That was some righteous shooting by the way."

"I just got lucky. He was distracted."

"And, now he's dead. My buddy said that freed up a lot of cops who've been trying to pin something on him for years. Anyway, it seems the feds were also interested in Mr. Hart."

"Since when did the FBI get interested in gas station stickups and local killings?"

"Well, other than the fact that this dirt bag was moving across state lines, there was his connection with the late Senator Longroux. It was actually Longroux the feds were more interested in; they just thought if they could roll Hart up, they'd get the big fish."

"Was this because of Longroux's activities here in DC?"

"Nah, they never tumbled to that. They were looking at him long before the shit started happening here. Seems there were some questions about strange things that kept happening to the senator's political rivals. One died in a strange boating accident, and another accidentally shot himself while cleaning his shotgun. Both deaths happened around the time the good senator was in a close race for reelection. They found out he had a connection with Hart, and put two and two together. Problem is, they never came up with the magic four. When the senator bought it, they dropped their investigation."

Kennedy shook his head. He took another sip of coffee. The liquid was lukewarm and tasted metallic. He pushed the cup away.

"So, with Longroux and Hart both dead, the feds and the cops down south are no longer concerned, right?"

"Right as rain. Not much to investigate when both suspects are already dead. The Alabama cops did have one interesting tidbit, though. Seems Longroux met Hart in Pass Christian,

Mississippi a couple of months before Lesley Carter was killed. Right after the meeting, our boy Hart dropped off their radar."

"That must be when Longroux brought him up here."

"That's what I figure. But, there's more. There were three people at the Pass Christian meeting. The boys in Alabama didn't make too much of it at the time. Longroux was always hanging around with the movers and shakers down there. But, when I pressed them on it, they faxed me the surveillance photos their guy took of the meeting. The fax wasn't all that clear, but I got a good one of the guy's face. You'll never guess who it was."

"I'm not good at guessing games," Kennedy said. "And, right now I'm not in the mood anyway."

"Aw, man, you're no fun at all." Kennedy started to stand. "Okay, okay, I know you got all this important international affairs shit to deal with. The third guy was none other than this old guy, Hitchcock you mentioned to me."

"Niles Hitchcock?"

"One and the same. Kind of makes you think, don't it?"

Yes it does, Kennedy thought, and none of the thoughts are good.

"It gets even better, though," Murphy continued. "I decided to do some checking on our friend Hitchcock. You know he was recently in Costa Rica. Went down there right after the senator's death. Well, I checked with the FBI and Immigration, and they show he just came back a few days ago. The FBI checked with their guy in the embassy down there, and there was a routine report of Hitchcock meeting a couple of times with some dude who is suspected of being involved in hit squads in one of them Central American countries."

"Shit." Was all Kennedy could say.

"The people down in Costa Rica lost track of both of 'em. They suspect this guy's somehow sneaked into the U.S."

"You got an ID on him?"

"Just a name and an old photo. Name's Ignacio Batista and it's rumored that he's responsible for more than a hundred killings – every one of 'em done personally."

"Holy crap! And, he's running around DC?"

"Now you see why I didn't want to wait for you to get to your office?"

Chapter Thirty-Two

Morgan had tossed and turned all night. No matter what he did sleep just refused to come in more than short, fitful snatches, inhabited by short clips of dreams that made him want to be awake. Sometimes he would be back in the fetid jungles of the Mekong Delta of Vietnam and the southeast part of Cambodia, with the stench of blood, feces, and mutilated flesh burrowing its way into his nostrils while the screams of the dying blanketed his ears. In other dreams, he found himself in a less exotic environment, what looked like a woodland park with hiking trails and camping areas. But, despite the peaceful looking environment, he sensed something dangerous lurking nearby. He could neither see nor hear it, but the hairs on the back of his neck were buzzing at high frequency, and he felt cold with fear.

He also dreamed about the phone call. After

his meeting with Chambers and Kennedy, Alison and Lee was how he was beginning to think of them, because other than Earline, they were the closest things to friends he had at the moment. Samuel Gosnell, the Dagastan desk officer, was nice enough, but Morgan wasn't quite ready to think of him as a friend – just not an enemy. He'd called the stranger back as had been suggested and said he would drop the idea of going to the union with his problem. He wasn't sure the man had believed him. He couldn't put his finger on it, but there was something in the way the man hesitated before speaking or maybe a tone in his voice that Morgan interpreted as skepticism. The man had made vague threats, but Morgan took them seriously. After all, people had already died in connection with the events in Dagastan half a world away.

Several times, he got up and made his way to the bathroom. He drank warm water from the tap, but instead of making him sleepy it only made him want to pee.

The dreams stopped around four-thirty, and after another thirty minutes of twitching and tossing about, he finally drifted off into a relatively untroubled sleep. Only to be jerked back to consciousness by the jangling sound of the phone.

He lay there for three rings, staring at the instrument. He was beginning to really dislike phones ringing in the early morning. On the fourth ring he picked it up.

"Yeah," he snarled into the mouthpiece.

"Mr. Morgan," Senator Appleby said. "Sorry to wake you so early. I wouldn't if I didn't think it important. You and I need to talk right away."

Morgan came fully awake. He hadn't placed Appleby yet, but he was beginning to think the man was at least not an enemy.

"Okay, senator," he said. "You need to give me time to get dressed and get a bite of breakfast, say an hour, then tell me where to meet you."

"Why don't you get yourself presentable and come on down to breakfast? I'm here in the lobby of your hotel."

Morgan hastily showered, shaved, and threw on a pair of khaki pants and a blue denim shirt. He found Appleby sitting on one of the overstuffed chairs in the front lobby. He was dressed in a cream colored suit with a bright red tie, and had on a pair of reddish-brown cowboy boots. A tan Stetson rested on his knees. He rose as Morgan approached and held out his hand.

"Thanks for seeing me, son," he said as he clasped Morgan's hands. "I hear they put on a nice spread for breakfast here. Why don't we retire to the dining room? We can talk over a plate of biscuits and gravy."

Appleby led the way to the dining room in the rear past the lobby. This early, there was only a yawning woman around whose job it was to ensure replenishment of the breakfast buffet table. They helped themselves to biscuits, slices of ham, scrambled eggs, home fried potatoes, fruit juice, and coffee.

They sat at a table in the back corner of the room, Morgan with his back to the wall where he had a good view of the entire room, but most importantly, could see anyone coming in. The senator sat across from him.

Appleby immediately began forking food into his mouth.

"Excuse my greediness," he mumbled around a mouthful of scrambled eggs. "But, ever since my wife died, I haven't had many opportunities for a proper breakfast. Most important meal of the day, you know."

Morgan ate slowly, watching the other man. He nodded and favored Appleby with a half-smile.

Appleby put his fork down.

"I know you want to know why in Sam hill I had to see you so early in the morning," he said. "But, you just sit there eating, and unlike most people you don't seem pushy about finding out."

"Like I told you at our last meeting, senator, I figure you'll tell me what you want me to know in your own good time."

"Dang it, son, I do like the cut of your jib. You're about the most plain-spoken bureaucrat I've ever met. Okay, let me tell you, but first, I need to give you a bit more background."

Appleby reiterated his involvement with the Committee.

"Now, we're made up of people from across the spectrum; politicians, bureaucrats, and people from industry. What unites us is a desire to see the country prosper."

"And, of course, you prosper as well," Morgan said.

"Touché, son. Sure; when the country does well, business ain't bad. Nothing wrong with that, long's you don't cross the line into illegal activity."

"What about immoral or unethical behavior?"

"Ah well, that's a whole other matter now ain't it. Morals and ethics are sometimes hard to define. I can say that there's not one war profiteer or arms merchant on the Committee. Our members tend to try and look for peaceful ways to settle things. Anyway, some time back I brought this fellow Niles Hitchcock into the Committee, figuring him being a veteran diplomat and all he'd bring an international view to our discussions. He's part of a group called the White Dragons."

"Who or what are the White Dragons?" Morgan asked.

"Near as I can figure, and I only have Niles' word on this, they're a bunch of Foreign Service Officers who feel they are the key to having a proper foreign policy, so they make themselves available to whatever administration gets elected."

"That's what the Foreign Service is all about."

"Yeah, but these fellows consider themselves a cut above. Niles once said to me that the rest of you don't count; you're only needed to make sure they are available when needed."

"That's a pretty elitist attitude," Morgan said.

"I take it you've never met Niles Hitchcock. He's the elitist, most stuck up bastard you're gonna meet in a month of Sundays, believe me."

"I've never met him, but the name's familiar. He did a lot of assignments to the White House before he retired."

"Among other things," Appleby said. "He's still able to pull strings over at State, with all his contacts."

You can say that again, Morgan thought. He knew now who it must have been on the phone. He didn't know how he knew, but he knew. Hitchcock probably had more moles in State than suburban lawns, which made him a dangerous man indeed.

"I know that worries you," Appleby said. "But, don't you fret about that. A U.S. Senator trumps a retired diplomat any day. You see, over on Capitol Hill we control the purse strings. Money talks. Of course, I got me a hunch old Niles can be dangerous in another way that I might not be able to help you with."

"You mean other than killing my career?"

"Yeah, I mean like killing *you*."

Morgan shuddered. Sure, people had been killed; of that he was aware; but, contemplating one's on mortality or eventual death is something the human brain doesn't take lightly to. Even with Appleby saying it so bluntly, it was hard for him to accept.

"What I don't understand," he said. "Is why a guy like Hitchcock would get himself involved in something like this. I mean, from what I've heard he had a pretty good career."

"How much do you know about this outfit you're a part of, son. I don't mean the technical stuff; what is you people call it – tradecraft? I mean the underlying history and culture of the

American diplomatic service?"

Morgan pondered the question for a few moments, realizing that he really knew precious little.

"Well, I know that what we know as the Foreign Service was established in 1924 when the separate Consular and Diplomatic Services were consolidated under the Rogers Act."

"That's right. Prior to that, the two were separate, and basically the diplomats were the wealthy and the consuls were business people. The consular guys survived on their fees, but since the diplomats couldn't really collect fees, only the rich could afford to do the job."

"I knew that."

"We have this tradition in this country that anyone can be a diplomat, as long as he or she – and, for the longest time it was only 'he,' – has the right connections. Hell, son, they didn't even have examinations for diplomats until 1906."

"That I didn't know."

"That's because after you pass the damn exam, they don't bother educating you. Not like I bet you remember when you were in the army. Now, they know how to do it; they educate and train you from enlistment to retirement. You learn the history, traditions and customs of the service. You go to work as an American diplomat; they teach you a language, show you which dessert spoon to use and kick your ass out the door."

Put that way, Morgan couldn't argue. That was the way the system worked. It seemed to work well most of the time. Sometimes, though, it was royally screwed up. He'd never made that connection before.

"So, why doesn't the president of congress do something about it?"

"Because it just isn't in our interest to fix it, that's why. Most presidents haven't trusted the professional diplomats, no matter what kind of high sounding speeches they make. They much prefer to put their own people in the positions that count. As for congress; well, son, we're politicians, and politicians need support, and we get a lot of that support by being able to hand out jobs to supporters. Long as you guys do what you do and don't complain, we're happy to let sleeping dogs stay in the dog house."

"That's awfully cynical. What about promoting the nation's interest, isn't that better done by well-trained professionals?"

"Sure it is. But, how many politicians really give a damn about national interest? They just want to get elected and stay in office – and, that goes for the politicians in the executive branch as well as those up where I work."

"When you put it like that, there doesn't seem to be much to be done about it."

"And, as long as there are enough of you that take that view, you're damn right. You think it's bad now, just hang around. I figure it'll get a hell of a lot worse. This town's always been about politics, but I smell a change in the political wind like you've wouldn't believe. It's beginning to get downright nasty."

"Is there no hope?"

"Well, I reckon we can hope it'll eventually sort itself out, or the voters will wake up and kick the bastards out on their kiesters. Of course, there will be those, like Niles Hitchcock and his cronies, that'll survive and even thrive no matter what happens, because they'll always do what's best for them and the rest of us be damned. Which brings me to why I *really* wanted to talk to you."

He'd shoved his plate aside and was fiddling with his coffee cup, only occasionally making eye contact with Morgan. A muscle in his right cheek fluttered.

"Niles came to see me the other day, and he was downright threatening. I'm not worried he'll get after me. He'd have to be crazy to try to do anything to a U.S. Senator, but you're a bit of a thorn in his side. So are a couple other people over at State, and I worry it might come after you. I can't prove it, but I have my suspicions he's done it before."

Morgan decided to trust the man. He couldn't say why; just a gut feeling.

"I received a threatening phone call, and I believe it was Hitchcock."

"Probably was, son," Appleby said. "You'd best be real careful."

"Unless he plans to shoot me from ambush, and I don't think he's capable of that, I think I can handle him."

"Yeah, but even someone with your military credentials might have a problem dealing with his friend. A real mean looking son of a bitch, a beaner from somewhere down there in Latin America name of Ignatius Batista or something like that. He had the look of a professional killer to me."

Morgan leaned forward, fixing Appleby in a steely gaze.

"Well, like I said, unless he plans to shoot me from ambush, I'll just have to take my chances."

It sounded good. Sounded brave as all get out. Real macho stuff. But, deep down inside Morgan knew he'd be in deep crap if a pro came after him. Time, he thought, to hook back up with the only person he knew in town who at least had a gun.

Chapter Thirty-Four

As soon as Appleby had gone, Morgan hotfooted it down to Foggy Bottom. He found Lee Kennedy at his desk, looking at a stack of papers.

Kennedy looked up as he walked in.

"What's up, Dave? You look like someone just kicked you in the balls."

Morgan related his conversation with Appleby.

"Shit," Kennedy said. "That pretty well puts a bow on it."

He then told Morgan about the information he'd gleaned from Al Murphy. At that point, Morgan looked down at the papers on his desk. On top of the stack was a grainy copy of a photo of Ignacio Batista. Something about the picture triggered a latent memory in Morgan's mind.

"Hey, that guy looks familiar," he said.

"This is Ignacio Batista, a hit man for some of the worst gangs in Latin America. He's reported to have been connected to a government death squad. He's thought to be somewhere in the DC area courtesy of our friend Niles Hitchcock."

"There's no reported to it," Morgan said. "I've seen that face before, and recently. I just can't remember where or when."

"How can you be sure? This is a faxed copy of a black and white photo. I mean, if you know what to look for, or you had the guy here you could compare –"

"No, I'm sure. Look, when I was doing patrols in Vietnam, one of the things that kept you alive was the ability to remember terrain features, landmarks; details, even the most insignificant, can be the difference between life and death. I don't like to brag, but I was pretty damn good at it. The best in my outfit in fact. I've seen this face before. Give me enough time and I'll remember where."

"Hey, I believe you, man," Kennedy said. "Until you do, though, we need to think about what we're gonna do to keep this guy from putting holes in us."

"I think we should include your friend Alison

in the discussion. She's in danger too."

"Yeah, you're right. Let's go to her office."

A few minutes later, they related the senator's warning to Chambers. When Morgan had finished talking, she just sat staring open mouthed at him for a long, long moment.

She then blinked and shook her head.

"What are we going to do?" she asked meekly.

"Well, for starters, none of us should go anywhere alone," Kennedy said. "Dave, I suppose you're safe in your hotel, but I'd avoid going out at night for now. As for you, young lady, I think you should come home with me."

"I'd planned to go on a picnic Saturday," Morgan said. "I really hate to completely disrupt my life because of a vague threat."

"I don't know, man," Kennedy said. "That's taking a big risk."

"I'm with Dave," Chambers said. "All we have is the senator's word anyway. I hate having my life turned upside down like this."

"The picnic's in a pretty public area," Morgan said. "Over at East Potomac Park. It'd be pretty hard for anyone to get close without being spotted. I'll make sure we're in an area that gives me good observation."

Kennedy shrugged. "I guess you've pretty much made up your mind, huh?"

Morgan shrugged. Was he being foolish, he wondered? Earline would understand if he postponed the picnic. He could tell from the look on Kennedy's face that he thought it was a foolish thing to do.

"I'll think about it," he said. "Let's see what happens today and tomorrow."

Kennedy looked over at Chambers.

"You're still coming home with me," he said.

Chapter Thirty-Five

Thursday, July 17, 1975, Washington, DC

The scene was familiar.

Two elderly white men walking down a hallway past an elderly black man with snow white hair who idly dusted tables, vases, and statues, completely unnoticed by the two white men. The black man, as the two passed and entered the room at the end of the hallway and closed the door behind them, moved softly and slowly to a position near the door. He didn't do anything as pedestrian as placing his ear against the door. He didn't have to. What only he knew was that any but whispered conversations inside the room were clearly audible in a spot near the door where the room's wall and the wall of the hallway came together.

It was like a movie loop that plays the same

In The Dragon's Lair

scene over and over again. Except that this time the sound track was different.

The man with a shock of white, neatly coiffed hair, wearing a tan suit with dark brown sequins on the shoulder, leaned forward. His face was suffused with blood; his capillaries threatened to erupt, and his eyes blazed. Senator Jonathan Appleby was supremely angry with the man he faced across the green felt covered table. The man, a slightly pudgy man with a fading tan on his liver spotted skin, was dressed in a dark blue suit with red power tie. His stringy white hair was combed across the top of his pate in a vain effort to cover a spreading bald spot. He looked back with a bland expression.

"Godammit, Niles," Appleby nearly shouted. "You've got to call off your dog. I know what you plan to do, and it's wrong, just plain wrong, and the Committee will not have it."

Niles Hitchcock, retired diplomat and senior member of the shadowy group known as the White Dragons, looked idly at his pudgy fingers, studying his fingernails. He finally looked up at Appleby, his expression a study of indifference.

"In the first place, Jonathan," he said quietly and evenly. "I'm not really sure you speak for the entire group. And, in the second place, I don't think you have the power, guts or balls to try and stop me. Plans are already in place, and

I see no reason to change them."

"Nonsense, man; there's always time to make changes, especially when what you plan to do is completely out of step with the Committee's philosophy."

"Is it?" Hitchcock leaned forward. His expression was that of a hunting animal that has cornered a helpless prey and is just about to pounce. "The politicians on the Committee want to get re-elected, right? The members from the business community are interested in continued profits? Do you really think they won't do whatever is necessary to achieve those goals?"

"I think they would stop short of killing people," Appleby said. "What you're planning to do is unthinkable and unconscionable."

"Oh, my dear Jonathan, you are so naïve. There's always been the need to sacrifice the few for the good of the majority. True leaders know this and are able to do it when necessary. A commander in combat has sometimes to sacrifice members of his organization for the greater good of the organization."

"How dare you compare what you're contemplating with what our military has to do in combat." Appleby was indignant, his cheeks flamed red. "You never served in uniform a day in your life."

Hitchcock laughed derisively. "One doesn't have to be a soldier to be in life or death situations. Right now, we're in a fight for the survival of our country. Our standing in the world plummeted after the Vietnam debacle. We're weak, and a weak America is not good for the world. We must do anything necessary to restore our position. If a few people must die for that to happen, it's regrettable, but in the long term inconsequential."

"But, David Morgan and the others are innocents."

"Hardly innocent, my dear fellow. Morgan, Kennedy and Chambers stand squarely in the way of getting done what needs to be accomplished. If they're not removed, all our efforts will have been for naught. In retrospect, I can see it was a mistake not to have them removed earlier."

"Like you had the others killed? You know, I still find it hard to believe that Carlton Longroux went along with you on this."

There was that harsh, mirthless laugh again. Hitchcock regarded Appleby with narrowed eyes.

"You know, at the end, he turned out to be as spineless as you. He developed a conscience, which, given what he'd had done to some of his political opponents back home was laughable."

He let it drop there, but Appleby knew what he'd just said, and he felt a shiver up and down his back; not just his spine, but his whole back felt as if it was the target of a hidden sniper. He recognized at that moment that Niles Hitchcock was indeed a dangerous person, and that he needed to tread carefully. The man had just said that his status as a United States Senator offered him no protection.

"I just wish you'd reconsider, Niles," he said. He made an effort to keep his voice even. "There has to be some other way to handle this situation."

"I'm not stupid, Jonathan. Don't you think I considered all the options? The circumstances are such that there is no other way to ensure the matter is laid to rest. Besides, once Ignacio has been sent out after a target, he tends to remain out of touch until he completes his assignment. I'm afraid there's no way I could stop things even if I wanted to."

Appleby knew the man was lying. But, there wasn't a damn thing he could do about it.

The meeting broke up. Hitchcock left first. He held his head high and walked with a purposeful stride. He was followed shortly by Jonathan Appleby. He walked with his shoulders slumped in defeat.

The elderly black man was sweeping both times, and both times, neither man paid him any attention.

When they'd gone, the old man leaned his broom in the corner and brushed some residual dust off his dark jacket and pants. He then went to a closet at the opposite end of the hall and removed a dark hat and placed it carefully over his white hair. For the second time in a week, he left the compound.

Chapter Thirty-Six

Saturday, July 19, 1975, East Potomac Park,
Washington, DC

Early Saturday morning Earline Brown picked Morgan up in a beat up 1969 cream colored Ford station wagon with fake wood paneling on the doors and sides. The car finish was more rust spot than cream paint, and the vehicle looked as if it would strain to make the in-town speed limit of 35 mph. A large picnic basket, umbrella, and a large green and white checked cloth were in the back of the vehicle.

"You didn't tell me you had a car," Morgan said as he settled himself into the passenger seat next to her.

"I don't drive this old thing except on weekends," she said. "Parking fees downtown cost more than it's worth, and it's too hard to find parking anyway."

Morgan lapsed into silence. Just sitting there looking at her as she aggressively manhandled the clunky vehicle through the Saturday morning traffic. The other drivers gave them a wide berth. He marveled at the contrasts in this woman. She was beautiful, of that there was no doubt, but she didn't flaunt it as some women did. She had a great sense of humor, and seemed to be compassionate. But, behind the wheel, her face was set in a mask of determination and almost homicidal anger as she muttered at the drivers who were slow moving away from her bucket of rust, cutting in front of some, and playing chicken with others to get them to drop back and let her change lanes. She was a completely different person.

"Aren't you worried about getting a ticket?"

"No," she said without looking at him. "They don't pay much attention to anybody but parking violators unless you hit someone."

Taking a deep breath, Morgan sat back in the seat, his hands gripping the sides tightly. He didn't resume breathing normally until they'd pulled into the parking area of East Potomac Park just off Ohio Drive, and she'd squeezed the station wagon into a space between a large sedan and a pickup. The space was so tight he had to remove the picnic supplies through the rear hatch. With the umbrella under one arm and the basket which was laden with food in his other hand, he followed her north past the golf course to a grassy area within sight of the bridge that spanned the park and river connecting DC with Northern Virginia.

Several groups of people were already there with their clothes spread out on the grass, some in the shade of the cherry trees that were planted along the sidewalk, some out in the open areas.

Morgan pointed out an area on a slope, one of the few sloped areas in the park that was a good hundred yards from any trees or plants large enough to conceal anyone. Even though he'd ignored Kennedy's advice to cancel the picnic, he wasn't taking any chances that someone would sneak up on them unawares. The area he chose had a clear view for a hundred yards or more in all directions.

He spread the cloth on the ground and set up the umbrella to block much of the sun's rays coming from the east. The sidewalk and the Washington Channel were in that direction, so he felt it was safe to do. As he helped Earline put the food on the cloth, he kept scanning the area, paying particular attention to nearby groups of people and a small copse of trees about a hundred yards to their north. Nothing he saw gave off warning vibes, but he didn't allow himself to relax. Brown didn't seem to notice his vigilance. She continued to chat away as she spread out the food and began placing it on two paper plates.

"I hope you like potato salad and fried chicken," she said. "I made lots. Spent most of last night fixing it."

"Love it," he said absently, still scanning the area.

"You don't sound too enthusiastic. I'll have you know I make the best potato salad on the east coast. And, the chicken is my grandmother's special recipe."

"Sorry. I'm sure it's delicious," he said. "I guess my mind was just wandering."

"That's not exactly the way to make a woman feel appreciated. Here I go to all this work fixing a meal for you, and you're sitting here thinking about another woman."

She cocked her head and gave him an inscrutable look.

"Oh no, I wasn't thinking about another woman. That would be impossible with you around. I was thinking about my current situation."

"You still worried about what personnel might do?"

He wanted to tell her that personnel was the least of his worries, and besides Senator Appleby had assured him that would be taken care of, but he wasn't sure how much he could tell her about the other things that were going on. He also didn't want to spoil the day by scaring her witless with stories of assassins skulking about planning to kill him.

"Yeah, I guess I am," he lied. "They haven't shown any inclination to be sympathetic, and I think they're looking for a scapegoat for the ambassador's death."

"Surely they don't think that was your fault."

"Who knows what they really think," he said, shrugging. "They didn't really seem interested in what happened out there, and . . . well, there are a few things I didn't feel like telling them, because they wouldn't want to hear them."

She leaned forward, placing her slender hand on his forearm.

"Things like what, David?"

He gazed into her dark brown eyes. They seemed to draw him inward and down into their depths. The emotions that he'd bottled up inside since that night when he was convinced Robert Ellingsworth had set him up to be killed poured out like water from a busted main. He told her his suspicions, holding back the current threat on his life. When he'd finished, he felt drained, but relieved; a great burden had been lifted from his soul.

She squeezed his arm gently.

"My goodness, what you've been through," she said. "No wonder you're so moody sometimes. And here I thought it was me."

The way she so deftly deflected his gloominess, taking in what he'd had to say, showing the appropriate sympathy nonverbally with the touch of her hand, and then suddenly making light of it amazed him.

"It's definitely not you," he said. "Heck, Earline, you're just about the only nice thing about this town right now."

"What about my friend Alison and her boyfriend?"

"Well . . . yeah, them too. But, you're nice in a completely different way."

"So, you ready to eat some of my chicken now and show proper appreciation?"

Happy for a change of subject, Morgan took the cold drumstick she proffered and bit into it. She was right, he thought, she's a damn good cook. The leg was crisp on the outside, soft on the inside, and spiced so that there was just a touch of zing to it as he chewed. She watched him eat with an expectant look on her face.

He finished the drumstick by biting off the end of the bone and sucking out the marrow. He then dropped the mangled bone on the edge of his plate and wiped his greasy fingers on the front of his shirt.

"Oh no, don't do that," Brown said in horror. "You'll never get the grease stains out."

"Doesn't matter," he said. "This is an old shirt. Besides, the grease spots will be there to remind me of the best darn chicken I've ever had."

She made a derisive snorting noise, but the darkening of her cheeks told Morgan that his compliment had hit home. He relaxed, but only to a degree. That part of him that had been forged in the heat of combat in the mountains, jungles, and swamps of Vietnam stayed on alert. He continued to scan the surroundings for anything remotely out of place.

Between the two of them, they made significant inroads into consuming the food she'd packed, which included ten drumsticks, a quart of potato salad, a quart of lemonade, and half a dozen biscuits with cheese and jelly. She'd also packed a bunch of dark purple grapes. When she lifted the fruit from the basked, Morgan smiled.

"Ah, so you will feed me grapes like the old Roman emperors had, eh?"

He leaned back on his elbow and looked down his nose at her.

"Don't press your luck, buster," she said. She pulled a grape from the bunch and tossed it at him.

As he ducked his head to try and catch the fruit several things happened.

Out of the corner of his eye, he saw the flash of light off metal in a little stand of trees about a hundred yards to his northwest. He felt the pressure of something zipping past his face, and a geyser of dirt and grass erupted some ten yards past him to his southeast.

His brain processed what happened almost unconsciously. Even though there'd been no sound, he knew with the certainty borne out of many months in combat that he'd just been shot at, that in fact, had he not ducked his head to try and catch the grape Earline Brown was tossing to him, a slug would have bored into his skull.

He reached across and grabbed Brown by the arms and pulled her toward him. Her eyes opened in surprise, and she started to smile until he pulled her, not into his lap, but onto the ground, where he then shielded her as he rolled the two of them down the incline.

When they'd come to rest, he lifted his head and saw that he could no longer see the trees which meant that whoever was in those trees could no longer see him. Brown's smile had been replaced by a confused frown.

"What was that all about?" she asked.

It was no longer possible to keep things from

her.

"Someone just shot at us," he said.

Her eyes went wide.

"Shot at, as with a gun? I didn't hear a shot."

He nodded.

"Whoever it is used a silencer. He's in that clump of trees just to the north of us."

"How do you know this?" she asked. "And, how do I know you weren't just using that as an excuse to manhandle me?"

"Earline, I only manhandled you as you put it to get you out of the line of fire. Besides, I don't manhandle women. If I'd wanted to hug you, or anything else, I would have been a bit smoother with it."

"Well, I certainly hope so."

She was taking the whole thing well. That might have been due to her not fully believing they'd actually been shot at, but Morgan didn't think so. She was one together woman.

"So, what do we do now?" she asked.

"Well, we're in a bit of a standoff. He can't come closer without exposing himself, but we're sort of trapped here."

"If he used a silencer, the other people here probably don't even know anything's happened," she said.

And then, Morgan had an idea. If the shooter wanted to remain out of sight, he'd have to divert attention in his direction.

"There's a guy with a gun in those trees over there," he shouted.

This caused an immediate reaction. Couples and groups all over the grassy area started screaming and running in all directions, a few even running toward the copse of trees. Morgan eased up the incline and peered over. He saw a scene of pandemonium, with people running to and fro, adults snatching up curious children who were curious about the commotion, others grabbing at their picnic supplies, and some just running hell bent for leather toward the parking lot. One figure, though, caught his attention. A man in dark clothing was strolling casually north from the vicinity of the trees, heading for the park exit in that area. Morgan smiled and breathed a sigh of relief.

"What's happening?" Brown asked quietly.

"I think we spoiled his plans," he said. He waited a few more minutes until the figure was out of sight. "I think it's okay now. Let's get out stuff and get the hell out of here. You wait right there while I retrieve things."

He eased up the incline and quickly folded the ground cloth, took down the umbrella and dragged them and the picnic basket down to where Brown still lay watching wide-eyed.

"You sure are calm for someone who just got shot at," she said. "My heart's beating a mile a minute."

"Not much point in getting excited when the shooting's stopped. Especially if you're still alive."

She laughed. "It's pretty hard to get excited if you're dead."

He gave her a quick hug, and, keeping his own body between hers and the north end of the park, quickly urged her toward the parked station wagon. Once inside the vehicle, he told her to just drive, not stopping near the north end of the park just in case the shooter was lying in wait for them. Once out of the park, he had her cross the Fourteenth Street Bridge, not into the District, but into Northern Virginia. For the moment, Morgan felt there would be safety in numbers.

Chapter Thirty-Seven

Kennedy and Chambers were sitting in his living room when they heard the rattle of an ancient motor outside. Looking outside, he saw an old cream colored Ford Station wagon pulling into his driveway.

Morgan and Brown were just getting out of the vehicle when he opened the door. He could see even from nearly twenty feet away that they both looked harried.

"Hey, guys, how was the picnic?" he called.

"Someone shot at us," Brown said with a trembling voice.

"Wha-"

"I'll tell you all about it," Morgan said. "As long as you don't say "I told you so.""

Once inside the living room Morgan

recounted the events that had transpired in the park.

"Good grief," Kennedy said when he'd finished. "You both could have been killed."

"Tell me about it," Morgan said. "If I hadn't been moving my head at that moment, the shot would have caught me square in the face."

Brown shuddered at the thought.

"Damn," Kennedy said. "We can't let this go on this way. We have to do something."

"Yeah, but what?" Morgan asked.

Just then, the phone rang. Kennedy picked it up. It was Al Murphy.

"Al, my friend Dave Morgan was just shot at in East Potomac Park," he said. "I think Niles Hitchcock might be behind it."

"You're probably right," Murphy said. Then he told him about an anonymous phone call he'd gotten relating Hitchcock's meeting with another man whom the caller wouldn't identify. The caller did say, though, that he'd heard Hitchcock say he was planning to have Kennedy, Chambers and Morgan killed.

"So," Kennedy said. "Are you going to pick Hitchcock up?"

"Damn, I wish I could. But, with nothing but an anonymous call to go on, he'd be back on the street before I could finish booking him, and that would make it hard to go after him again."

"What the hell can we do then?"

Kennedy was feeling frustrated and angry.

"If there was only some way we could get Hitchcock and his gunman in the same place, and somehow get him to implicate himself," Murphy said. "But, I got a feeling he's too smart for that."

"Maybe not," Kennedy said. He put his hand over the phone and turned to Morgan. "Dave, you still got the number of the guy who called and threatened you?"

Morgan nodded.

"I think that guy's Hitchcock. You willing to take one more risk if it gives us a chance to nail him?"

"If it puts this son of a bitch away, damn right I am," Morgan said.

"David, you can't put yourself at risk again," Brown said. She laid a hand on his arm, her eyes wide with alarm.

"I'm at risk as long as Hitchcock's running loose," he said. "Worse, everyone around me is at risk as well. It has to stop." He turned to Kennedy. "What do you have in mind?"

Kennedy took his hand away from the phone

and explained his plan to Morgan with Murphy listening.

"It's a long shot," Murphy said, when he'd finished. "But, it just might work."

"I'll have Dave make the call, and then I'll tell you where and when," Kennedy said and rang off. "Okay, Dave, you up for this?"

"Give me the phone," Morgan said. There was steel in his voice.

He dialed the number from memory. After three rings, a cultured voice answered.

"Yes?"

"Mr. Hitchcock, this is David Morgan," Morgan said. "We have to talk?"

There was a long moment of silence on the other end.

"Well, Mr. Morgan," Hitchcock said. "I must say, you live up to your reputation. How did you know?"

"It doesn't matter. I know. Now, we have to meet and talk before things get really out of hand."

"I'm afraid I really don't know what you're talking about, Mr. Morgan. Things seem to be going much as one would expect them to go."

Morgan's face tightened. Watching him,

Kennedy could sense what he was thinking, even though he couldn't hear the other end of the conversation. The man was just about at the end of his patience. He made a slight shaking motion of his head and smiled. Cool it, David, he thought. We can get this guy. Just don't let him rattle you.

Morgan took a deep breath, and seemed to settle down.

"Whatever," he said. The steel was back in his voice. "Let's meet anyway so there's no misunderstanding."

He gave the meeting details over the phone. Kennedy watched as he nodded, and then saw a smile light up his brown face. Morgan hung up the phone and turned to face him, his smile broader now.

"He bought it," he said. "The meeting's on for day after tomorrow."

Chapter Thirty-Eight

*Monday, July 21, 1975, Roosevelt Island, District
of Columbia*

The weekend had been quiet, but busy, as
Kennedy worked with Al Murphy to set the trap
in place for Niles Hitchcock and his confederate.
He'd suggested Theodore Roosevelt Island, a
wooded island in the Potomac River near the
Virginia shore, as the meeting place. Close
enough to river bank below Rosslyn that it's
almost possible to jump onto it, most people
think the island is part of Virginia, but the with
the oddities of the way the District's boundaries
are drawn, it's actually part of the District of
Columbia.

As part of the national park system, law
enforcement on the island is primarily the
responsibility of the U.S. Park Police. Murphy
coordinated with the Park Police station seven
miles west of the island along the George

Washington Memorial Parkway.

Morgan thought Kennedy's suggestion of the island as a venue was a stroke of genius. Hitchcock would know of Kennedy's relationship with the DC police, and would, like most people, assume the island was in Virginia, so it would be difficult to bring the Arlington County police in to disrupt the meeting. In fact, given the evidence they had, it would be impossible. With luck, he thought, Hitchcock wouldn't think about the Park Police.

The meeting had been arranged for 4:00 pm, just two hours before the normal closing time, which minimized the number of innocent bystanders in the event of gunfire – and, Morgan feared there would in fact be gunfire, because he couldn't see the Latin American gunman meekly surrendering.

Morgan hadn't told Hitchcock that Kennedy would be accompanying him to the meeting, but since the man's plan was to kill them both anyway, he figured that wouldn't be a problem. The problem would be to try and forestall the shooting until they could get him to say something incriminating.

It all looked so easy in the movies, but all day on Sunday, Morgan sat on Kennedy's living sofa – Kennedy had insisted that he and Earline Brown stay with him until they caught Hitchcock – pondering how he could get

Hitchcock to confess to his crimes before the man ordered his hired gun to kill him.

There had been a long argument on Saturday when Morgan asked if Kennedy had an extra sidearm that he could let him have. Kennedy had reminded him that DC had strict gun laws, and he'd be putting himself in danger of arrest if he was caught with a weapon. Morgan had held firm, though, maintaining that it was better to risk arrest on a gun charge than get gunned down because he couldn't defend himself. Finally, Kennedy let him have a .38 police special that he used as a backup on occasion.

"Just don't pull this thing unless you absolutely have to," he warned. "Not only could you be arrested for having it, but I could be in trouble for giving it to you."

"Don't worry," Morgan said. "I'll only show it if I plan to use it. I've handled guns before, you know."

"I know, but combat's not the same as being on the streets of DC."

"After getting shot at you could have fooled me. It felt a lot like being back in combat."

That silenced Kennedy. The situation they faced was a lot like combat. And, if they were to survive, Morgan thought, they'd have to fight back just as if they were in a war zone.

The really complicating factor they'd faced during the weekend was sleeping arrangements. None of the adults would even think of evicting Rachael from her room, but with her present, boy-girl, boy-girl sleeping arrangements were out of the question. Eventually, Chambers came up with the suggestion that she and Brown take the remaining bedroom and the two men sleep in the living room. That led to a debate between Morgan and Kennedy over which one would take the couch, with Kennedy insisting that Morgan, as his guest, take the couch. Morgan, though, would have none of it, so both men ended up sleeping on folded blankets on the floor.

On Monday, Kennedy and Chambers called in and informed their respective offices that they would be taking a day of annual leave, claiming upset stomachs from too much weekend celebration. Since neither of them had a reputation of abusing vacation time, no questions were asked.

They then spent the day with Morgan and Kennedy going over the plan for meeting with Hitchcock.

At 2:30, Murphy called to inform them that the Park Police, augmented by several members of DC's SWAT Team, were in place. Their plan was to arrive thirty minutes early so they could wait for Hitchcock, and it was only a ten minute drive from Kennedy's house to Rosslyn and

Roosevelt Island, so there was little for them to do but sit around and wait.

Morgan found the waiting to be the hardest part. It had always been that way for him. Waiting to go out on patrol. Waiting in a position for an expected enemy attack. Waiting in an ambush site for an enemy target to appear. The waiting, the anticipation, the not knowing what will happen next is always the worse part of a soldier's life. Combat is like a suspended interval of time, when everything slows down and speeds up at the same time, the sense of hearing is heightened and your muscles and brain flip into automatic pilot mode. True thinking is minimized. You mostly think in brief spurts. Duck. Incoming. I'm hit. Enemy at nine o'clock. When the shit's hit the fan, there's no time for long speeches or profound thoughts.

At 3:00, Morgan and Kennedy ate ham sandwiches washed down with unsweetened ice tea and began preparing for their journey to Roosevelt Island. Morgan tucked the .38 into the left side of his belt and pulled his shirt out so that it hung over it, concealing the weapon from all but the most careful observer. Kennedy put his 9mm Glock in a shoulder holster and then put on a light windbreaker. They said their goodbyes to Rachael and the two worried-looking women and piled into Kennedy's car.

Kennedy drove to US Route 50, exited near the back entrance to Fort Myer and then past the Arlington National Cemetery main entrance to George Washington Memorial Parkway, heading north. At the entrance to Roosevelt Island, he pulled in and parked in a vacant spot at the north end. They got out and crossed the pedestrian bridge to the island itself.

In his phone call with Hitchcock, Morgan had told him the meeting place would be just past the woods trail and upland trail at the south end of the island, at the beginning of the swamp trail. Any late visitors would likely be at the Memorial Plaza near the entrance, so this, he'd reckoned, would give them privacy. Mainly, he felt this would remove any hazard to innocent bystanders should things go bad, and he always planned for the worst case.

Theodore Roosevelt Island is covered with oak, maple, cedar and pines, with a profusion of low-lying bushes and tangled vines in the dark gray earth. The network of trails that encircle and cross the island are hard packed gray earth, except for the swamp trail on the eastern side, which has a number of wooden bridges spanning marshy areas, with the rest being darker gray, perpetually wet earth that squishes beneath your feet as you walk.

They'd only gone a few yards before the sound of traffic on the parkway was muted by the trees. To Morgan it was eerily like many of the patrols he'd been on in Vietnam, with nothing but the sound of air brushing the leaves, the chirp of insects, and the sound of your own breathing.

He knew from the sound of his footfalls on the soft earth when they reached the beginning of the swamp trail at the south end of the island. Thick growths of trees and brush surrounded them. Ahead, about ten yards, was the first of the low wooden bridges, little more than elevated slat sidewalks hanging suspended just inches above the fetid water and mud of the swamp that covered most of this side of the island.

As they neared the bridge, two figures appeared around the bend and walked to the far end of the bridge. Morgan recognized the Hispanic looking man as Ignacio Batista. From the distance, he looked exactly like the photo Kennedy had shown him. Next to him was an elderly man with mottled flesh and thin white hair – Niles Hitchcock. The two men stopped at the bridge, staring at Morgan and Kennedy as they approached the opposite end.

"Mr. Hitchcock, I presume," Morgan said.

"And, I'm guessing your friend is Ignacio Batista," Kennedy said. "Immigration would love to know he's here."

Hitchcock cleared his throat. Batista glared at Kennedy.

"I'd figured you might come alone, Mr. Morgan," he said. "But, then, I guess it's okay that you're both here. Now, why did you want to meet with me?"

"For starters," Morgan said. "I'd like you to call off your dog here. He tried to shoot me Saturday. Fortunately for me he's a lousy shot."

"You are alive only because you moved at the last moment," Batista spat.

"Shut up, Ignacio," Hitchcock said.

Batista's face reddened and his lips turned down in a snarl.

Morgan smiled. Almost there. Just have to keep them talking. He kept his hands loose at his side, his fingers hooked under the hem of his shirt.

"You have no reason to fear us," Morgan said. "All we want is to be left alone."

"I don't fear you," Hitchcock said. "But, you are an impediment to some very important plans. I wish that I could take your word that you only want to be left alone. But, I know people like you two and the lovely Miss Chambers; you can't resist riding to the rescue, trying to solve puzzles. Your nosiness, and that of others, has already created problems for us."

"Who is us?" Kennedy asked. "The moles you have burrowed in the State Department?"

"Mole is such a pejorative term. I prefer to think of the people who support us as patriots who want to see our nation resume its rightful place in the world, and who are willing to ally themselves with like-minded people."

"And, those who don't support you, like Lesley Carter," Kennedy went on, trying to goad the man. "You get rid of, right?"

Hitchcock cocked his head to one side, regarding Kennedy warily. Morgan feared that his friend might have gone too far, but then, Hitchcock chuckled mirthlessly.

"Ah yes, I'd forgotten about the unfortunate Miss Carter. Too curious and too stubborn for her own good she was. A tragic, but unavoidable sacrifice for the overall good of the cause I'm afraid."

"Just what the hell *is* your cause?" Morgan asked. "You try to play footsy with a man who overthrows the government in a region where you have to know the Russians aren't going to stand idly by while we mess around. What did you hope to achieve by that?"

An indignant look crossed Hitchcock's face.

"That could have worked. I think Ellingsworth probably overplayed his hand. Even as a junior officer, when I first recruited him for the White Dragons, he was a bit over-ambitious. I jokingly told him once that it would be the death of him. I guess I was right."

Morgan and Kennedy had stopped just short of the bridge. The ground to either side of the trail at their end looked moist, but solid. At the far end it looked as soupy as thick soup for a good distance back from the trail that wound through the trees. He wondered where the police Kennedy had promised had concealed themselves. The vegetation was thick, but there didn't appear to be many solid places to stand or crouch. He'd been discretely scanning the bushes and trees to the side and front, looking for some signs, but had seen nothing. If it hadn't been for his trust in the security agent, he would have been convinced that they were here facing Hitchcock and his hired killer alone.

The signal Kennedy had given him was the phrase, 'so, you had all those people killed,' which would alert the police to move in. Hitchcock's answer to the question was irrelevant. He'd already as much as confessed to having the desk officer Lesley Carter killed, and being involved in Ellingsworth's activities in Dagastan. He could sense Kennedy looking at him out of the corner of his eye. The man was probably wondering why he didn't give the signal. He knew he should, but there were still some things he was curious about.

"These White Dragons have been coming up since this mess started," he said. "What, or who the hell are they?"

"Not that it will do you any good to know, Morgan," Hitchcock said. "But, we are a group of dedicated senior diplomats who make ourselves available to our government whenever we're needed. We have a few retired people who can do special envoy roles, and those on active duty to fill positions in the administration."

"But, that's what the entire Foreign Service is for," Morgan protested.

"No administration has ever fully trusted the service," Hitchcock said. "And, for good reason. Most of you are worried about being balanced, covering all sides of an issue, telling it like you see it on the ground. Politicians don't want that. They want people who will carry out their mandate without question. People who will tell them what they want to know."

"In other words, you pander to the politicians in order to get good jobs. What about what's good for the country?"

Hitchcock shrugged.

"I admit from time to time, we get politicians elected who aren't the best. But, they don't last long. Pretty soon, the people elect someone else. By being available to serve faithfully whoever is elected, we do benefit the country."

"How in hell can you call shaping your message to fit the desires of the listener helping the country? They need to have the truth, even if they don't like it. That's how you help the country."

"That, my young friend, is why you would never be a candidate for the organization. You sound like my good friend Senator Appleby; all mom and apple pie. The world doesn't work that way, and it's people like me that understand that and are most capable of dealing with it. Everyone else has to either stay in the background or be moved out of the way."

"Like all the people you've had killed," Morgan said. Now was the time. "So, you had all those people killed."

From that point, for Morgan, seemed to happen in slow motion. To his left and right, he saw what he'd thought were clumps of bushes suddenly become uniformed police officers in riot gear, pointing their weapons at Hitchcock and Batista and shouting for them to 'drop their weapons and get down on the ground with their hands outstretched in front.' At the same time, he saw Batista reach behind him and start swinging a large, black pistol in his general direction. To his right, he sensed more than saw Kennedy drop to one knee, drawing his own weapon, while he was dropping to his left, yanking the left side of his shirt aside as he reached for the .38 stuck in his belt.

Batista almost had his weapon on line when Morgan squeezed off a shot in a two handed grip as he fell forward, his elbows planted in the soft earth. He heard a loud bang to his immediate right – Kennedy letting go with two shots. Batista's arm stopped in mid-swing, and he rose up on tiptoe as three slugs in rapid succession slammed into his right shoulder, upper right chest and left chest. He shook his head and resumed his effort to aim his weapon at Morgan and Kennedy.

There was another shout from Morgan's right.

"Drop the weapon and get down on the ground."

Batista ignored it. Hitchcock was cringing and inching back down the trail. Suddenly, there was a sound like firecrackers going off from Morgan's right and left. Batista's body jiggled like a poorly manipulated marionette, and then plunged backwards off the bridge. It made a large splash as it hit the murky, muddy water, and quickly sank beneath it, disappearing from view. Hitchcock whirled to run.

"Stop where you are," a loud voice commanded. "Or, we will shoot you."

Hitchcock froze in place, his arms in the air.

Several cops ran forward across the bridge. One handcuffed Hitchcock and manhandled him back to where Morgan and Kennedy were now standing and brushing dirt from their clothing. The others found sticks and poked around until they found Batista's body, and then they hauled it out of the water and on to the trail where they lay him on his back.

Al Murphy walked up to Morgan and Kennedy.

"That was some shooting for a civilian," he said to Morgan.

Morgan looked down guiltily at the .38 in his hand.

"Uh –"

Murphy reached over and gently took the weapon. He turned to Kennedy.

"I'm assuming this belongs to you?"

"Uh, yeah," Kennedy said.

Murphy handed it to him.

"That was some neat two-handed shooting, Lee; real neat." He looked around. "Don't worry, I'll talk to the Park Police, and that's the story that will be in the record."

He held his hand out to Morgan.

"Off the record, that was a pretty good shot," he said.

The two men shook hands. After releasing

his hand, Murphy patted him on the shoulder.

"What happens now?" Morgan asked.

"Well, we heard Hitchcock pretty much confess to having Lesley Carter killed. That alone will get him a long stretch. I imagine once we start sweating him, he'll cough up more. The immigration boys will be happy to know we got Batista too."

"So, it's finally over?"

"For you guys it is," Murphy said. "For me, it's just getting started." He turned to Kennedy. "Why don't you two go on and get out of here. You can come to the station tomorrow and make your statements."

Chapter Thirty-Nine

*Thursday, July 24, 1975, The Lincoln Memorial,
Washington, DC*

It actually took the better part of the following two days for Morgan and Kennedy to give their full statements. After Hitchcock's arrest was announced, the FBI decided that he was a person of interest into their ongoing investigation of political corruption, and had the two of them in FBI headquarters in downtown DC for three hours of intensive interviews.

Finally, though, it was all in the past, and Morgan could concentrate on getting out from under the rock personnel was holding over his head.

He'd just come out of the shower on Thursday morning when the phone rang. It was Jonathan Appleby.

"Why don't you meet me down at the Lincoln

Memorial at 10:00 this morning, son?" Appleby said. Morgan agreed and the senator broke the connection.

Morgan arrived at the memorial at ten minutes before the hour. Appleby, dressed in a light brown suit, a beige shirt with dark brown string tie, reddish brown cowboy boots, and a wide-brimmed white Stetson, was standing at the base of the marble steps waiting for him. Several groups of tourists slowed as they walked past him, some pointing and not a few snapping pictures of him as if he was part of the Mall's exhibits. For his part, Appleby just stood there with a broad smile on his face, in a 'valiant frontiersman looking west' pose. As Morgan walked up his smile broadened.

"I like a man who believes in being on time, or early," Appleby said, extending his hand. "That was some excitement you and Mr. Kennedy had the other day."

"That it was," Morgan replied. "But, it put an end to Niles Hitchcock's reign of terror at least."

Appleby frowned. He laid a hand gently on Morgan's shoulder.

"Let's move up to the top of the steps," he said. "So we're closer to the Great Emancipator as we talk." Morgan followed him up the steps, their shoes making clicking sounds as they ascended. At the top, Appleby found a shadowed place on the low marble wall and sat.

He patted the space beside him. "Take a load off, David."

Morgan sat, not touching the man, but close enough that he could feel the heat radiating from his body.

Appleby looked up at the large statue of Lincoln sitting gazing pensively out over the Mall.

"I think this is a most appropriate place for you and I to talk, son," he said. "Here under the watchful eye of the Great Emancipator."

David looked up at the statue.

"Yes, he is at least partially responsible for a lot of the progress we've made in this country in the past century."

"Oh, I don't mean that," Appleby said. "Although, the emancipation was a policy that was long overdue, and the right way for the country to go. No, I'm talking about his success in keeping this country from fragmenting. Can you imagine what history would be like if the south had stayed out of the Union?"

"Well, we certainly would never have become a world power," Morgan said. "And, I guess we'd have been easy pickings for some of the European powers who had their eyes on our resources."

"Absolutely right. Now, son, to this problem

of yours," Appleby continued. "I know you think it's over; and, as far as Niles Hitchcock is concerned, well I reckon it is. But, don't ever forget this one thing; in this town there's always someone willing to sacrifice the common good for the sake of his ego or some foolish cause. It's just a matter of time until another Niles Hitchcock surfaces."

"That's a frightening thought," Morgan said.

"It's meant to be. It's meant to keep you on your guard. Son, it's people like you and me that are the hope for this country. People who are willing to put the country first, and who are willing to stand vigil to guard against those who would do it harm through selfishness."

"Gosh, senator, there's not much I can do at my level."

Appleby patted Morgan's knee.

"As an individual, maybe not, but there are a few thousand of you Foreign Service Officers serving all over the world, and you're in a position to shape what our politicians and leaders know about the world. Your duty is to make sure they get the truth, the unvarnished truth, and not some watered-down version to make them feel good. As you rise through the system, you've got to support those below you and keep filling the institution with true professionals."

"Sure, I understand that's one of my duties as a professional. But, how much clout do we really have in the long run?"

"Given the lack of trust every presidential administration has shown you people, only a little. And, frankly that will diminish with time as they put more and more political hacks at lower and lower levels in your system. They'll overwhelm you with numbers. The only way you can deal with that is to make sure you become the most professional, capable institution out there."

Morgan made a snorting noise.

"There's the problem," he said. "I haven't noticed that we're particularly good at providing professional education; at least, not the kind I was accustomed to in the army. Our attitude seems to be, they're educated when they pass the test and we hire them, they don't need any more education."

"That, son, is the blind spot that has to have some light shone on it. No matter how smart you might be the day you start a job, if you don't keep your skills up through education, training, *and* practice, you're gonna get rusty."

"Try telling that to our senior people who look at anything other than language training as a waste of time and a danger to your career because it keeps you out of the normal work rating cycle."

"I don't know what to tell you there," Appleby said. "I mean, we could pass legislation dictating a certain amount of training and education, but the bureaucracy always finds a way around any law it doesn't like, and besides, that kind of decision is best made by the people most directly affected by it."

"A vicious cycle," Morgan said, his shoulders slumped. "The very people who need it don't think they need it, so they refuse to do it, which further weakens them. It's like a man who can't swim who keeps wading toward deeper water."

"Well, at least you'll be able to get back into the fight and do your part. And, I expect to hear great things about you in the coming years."

Morgan's eyes went wide.

"Do you mean –"

"That's right, son," Appleby said. "That little personnel problem of yours no longer exists. You'll be getting a call any day now to get your tail back out to Dagastan and back to work"

"I don't know how to thank you, senator. How on earth did you do it?"

"Well, I had to wave the budget to get their attention, but that works every time. Then, after they stopped squawking and making excuses, and told me the details of what they were doing, I made a few suggestions, which they were all too willing to accept, because it makes this whole thing go away."

"Ellingsworth's role in this won't be brought up will it?"

"That, son, is up to you. I suspect that role was nothing to be bragging about."

"Yes, but it serves no purpose to tarnish the man's name at this stage," Morgan said. "Of course, I do worry about Vera Cotton, his secretary. She was devoted to him, and it was her allegations that started this whole mess."

"I wouldn't worry about her, if I was you. She'll be busy getting herself settled in her new job in Bermuda. I think a few weeks in the island sun, she'll forget all about Mr. Ellingsworth."

Morgan laughed. Suddenly, he felt relieved. A sack of stones had been lifted from his shoulders. There would be, he knew, career obstacles in the future, but for now things were back to normal. Appleby had pushed the right buttons and pulled the right levers as only an experienced Washington power broker could. Morgan was grateful, and he thanked the senator profusely, but as he walked away from the memorial, from beneath Abraham Lincoln's stern gaze, he was determined not to become a part of the system that the senator so comfortably inhabited.

Chapter Forty

Friday, July 25, 1975, Francis Scott Key Hotel,
Washington, DC

Things had indeed gone as quickly as Senator Appleby had predicted. Morgan had a phone message waiting for him when he got back to his hotel. The personnel inquiry had concluded, and it was determined that what had happened was an 'unfortunate accident' that no one could have foreseen or avoided. He was cleared for immediate return to duty. So much for it not having been an adversarial process, he thought.

As soon as he finished talking to some low level clerk in personnel, he called Samuel Gosnell who informed him that he had reservations on the late night flight the next night, Friday, out of Dulles Airport by way of Amsterdam. In two days he'd be back with his guys in Kazbektun.

He spent the rest of the day packing. Finally, around 4:00 he remembered he hadn't talked to Earline, so he called her. She informed him that her aunt who lived in Baltimore had fallen ill and she was driving up that evening, so she wouldn't be able to go out with him, putting the first dark spot on the brightness of his situation. He didn't complain, though, just promised to write her now and then, and telling her that he would be taking his next R&R in Washington, DC, so he hoped she could arrange her annual leave around the same time.

Not being able to see her put a slight damper on his mood, but with all that happened, he couldn't stay sad for long.

That night, he slept soundly and without disturbing dreams for the first time since the whole mess started.

On Friday morning, he woke early, double checked to make sure he'd packed everything, and after getting dressed in casual travel clothing, had a big breakfast.

He spent the rest of the day wandering around the Mall, visiting the monuments and museums, lingering a long time in front of the Lincoln Memorial, just staring up at the brooding figure of the Sixteenth President. Finally, around mid-afternoon, feeling the need to wash off the sweat of a day outside in the July heat, he went back to his hotel.

Inside the room, he stripped, leaving a trail of clothing from the door to the bathroom, and stepped under a lukewarm shower, just letting the water massage his body.

He wasn't sure how long he'd been standing in the shower when he heard the chime of the doorbell. Stepping out of the shower, he grabbed a towel and patted himself dry. He then wrapped the towel around his waist and padded to the door, prepared to tell whatever hotel service person it was that he was checking out in three hours, so go away until then.

His eyes went wide and his breathing stopped when he pulled the door open. Earline Brown, dressed in a white blouse with the top two buttons undone, and a pair of dark brown slacks that clung to every inch of her lower body, stood there, her smooth brown arms folded beneath her ample chest.

She eyed him up and down as he stood there with a moist bath towel loosely around his waist.

"Uh, Earline," he said. "I thought you were in Baltimore with your sick aunt?"

"Turned out she wasn't as sick as we thought. I might go back up this weekend, but I have another cousin who's covering for me now."

Her eyes stopped around his midsection.

Little spots of red blossomed on her cheeks.

"Uh, am I interrupting something important?" she asked, cocking her head to look past him into the room.

Morgan stepped to the side.

"No," he said. "I'd just been out walking around all day, and I thought I'd wash the sweat off before I go to the airport."

A strange smile crossed her face.

"You have three hours before you have to leave for the airport," she said.

"Sure, at least three, why?"

"That means you have time for another shower if it becomes necessary," she said.

As she walked past him into the room, she reached for the third button on her blouse.

Epilogue

Saturday, July 26, 1975, Washington, DC

United States Senator Jonathan Appleby, his string tie loosened and his cream colored jacket hung over the back of an adjacent chair, sat at an large round table in the red brick three story building that sat behind the high walls on a hill that elevated it slightly above the street and its neighbors. In one hand he held a crystal goblet that contained some expensive brandy. In the other he held an illegal Cuban cigar. Light blue smoke wafted from the end of the cigar, slowly toward the crystal chandelier suspended over the center of the table. The rich aroma of the cigar filled the room.

Appleby was alone except for the elderly black man who had maintained the place for as long as he could remember.

"Won't you join me in a brandy and cigar,

Benjamin?" Appleby said.

The man's brown face was impassive, as if it had been carved from mahogany.

"No thank you, sir," he said in his deep baritone voice. "I don't drink or smoke. I have myself a cup of coffee from time to time, but that's all."

Appleby drew on the cigar. When he exhaled, a cloud of smoke billowed around his head.

"How did you manage to go through life so long and collect so few vices?" he asked.

The black man pushed an ash tray closer to the senator.

"I just figures out what's right and what's wrong, and I try to avoid what's wrong," he said. "And, I always do my duty as best I can."

"If only life was that simple."

"Seems to me, sir," the old man said. "It is just that simple. No matter how hard or complicated your job is, there's right and there's wrong. And, even a complicated job has duties attached to it, doesn't it?"

Appleby looked at the man through the haze of cigar smoke.

"You know, Benjamin, I think you have a point. It is just a matter of trying to do the right thing, isn't it?"

"Yes, sir it is," the old man nodded. "The right thing done passably well beats the wrong thing done perfectly every time. You having lunch here today?"

"I believe I will. Something light."

"Will you be eating alone?"

"Yes, Benjamin, I will be eating alone today. I'll be out of town for the next six weeks. I imagine the next time the group meets here will be in September, so you should have some time off."

The old man nodded. He never took time off. His duty was to the house. But, he didn't need time off, really. What he treasured was time to himself, and if these old white men insisted on not working in July and August, that was fine with him.

"Thank you, sir," he said. He inclined his head slightly. "I'll go to the kitchen and fix you a nice light lunch."

Then, quietly, he turned on his heel and silently left the room. He moved so quietly and smoothly, he didn't even disturb the cloud of cigar smoke that hung in the air.

Titles by Charles Ray

Buffalo Soldier history series
Buffalo Soldier: Trial by Fire
Buffalo Soldier: Homecoming
Buffalo Soldier: Incident at Cactus Junction
Buffalo Soldier: Peacekeepers
Buffalo Soldier: Renegade

Other fiction
Angel on His Shoulder
She's No Angel
Child of the Flame
Pip's Revenge
Wallace in Underland
Further Adventures of Wallace in Underland: Wallace Saves the King
Dade Letter and Other Tales (a collection of short stories)
The White Dragons: A novel of international intrigue
In the Dragon's Lair

Nonfiction
Things I Learned from My Grandmother About Leadership and Life
Taking Charge: Effective Leadership for the Twenty-first Century
Grab the Brass Ring
African Places: A Photographic Journey Through Zimbabwe and southern Africa

Al Pennyback mysteries

Color Me Dead	*Memorial to the Dead*
Deadline	*Dead, White, and Blue*
A Good Day to Die	*The Day the Music Died*
Die, Sinner	*Deadly Intentions*
Death By Design	*Till Death Do Us Part*
Deadly Dose	*Dead Man's Cove*
Dead Men Don't Answer	*Death From Unnatural Causes*
Deadly Paradise	*Kiss of Death*

Get *The White Dragons*, the book that started it all!

Available in paperback and for Kindle.

Paperback - $14.71
Kindle Version - $6.95

Available at Amazon.com, Amazon.co.uk, and other retail book sites. This book, in both versions can also be ordered through the author's website: http://charlesaray.blogspot.com.

Chapter One of *The White Dragons*

Thursday, May 8, 1975, Washington, DC

Lesley Carter was worried.

First, she'd been held up by her boss, and feared she'd miss her bus. The L1 Metro bus arrived at the stop at Twenty-third and I Streets at 6: 40 pm, and was seldom late, nor did it wait long. If she'd missed it, she would have been looking at more than an hour wait for the next bus. She could take a cab for the 20-minute ride to her neighborhood, on Calvert Street, near the National Zoo, but didn't feel like paying the ten dollar fare.

She was breathing hard as she arrived at the already crowded corner, near Washington Circle, just north of George Washington University Hospital. She'd nearly run from the Department of State building's E Street side, fearing that her short legs wouldn't enable her to move fast enough. She found a clear spot near the front of the crowd and proceeded to pay her fellow commuters no mind; a small group that included several elderly black ladies in gray-green scrubs who worked at the hospital, a portly white businessman in a suit that was rumpled from his own walk in the humidity of mid-May in Washington, DC, three young men who looked like students from the university, and two girls in the plaid skirts and white blouses of a nearby private Catholic high school. She didn't notice the slender, narrow faced man with close set eyes and dark brown hair combed straight back from a high forehead, dressed in dark blue shirt and pants who had been behind her from the moment she crossed F Street, and who now took up a position at the rear of the crowd.

She was breathing hard from her walk, but a glance at the cheap Timex watch on her left wrist showed her that she'd made it with ten minutes to spare.

Despite not missing her bus, she still felt antsy. It had been a surreal day.

She was just settling into her first month on the job as desk officer for the tiny Central Asian country of Dagastan in the European Bureau of the Department of State. A grade 3 Foreign Service Officer, she was on her fourth tour, the first domestic assignment since finishing the orientation course and French language training seven years earlier. Getting the desk officer slot had been a surprise; she was a consular officer, and would normally been assigned to the Bureau of Consular Affairs upon return to the U.S., but, in her last posting, at the U.S. Embassy in Dakar, Senegal, she'd been assigned to the political section's most junior position with responsibility of reporting on activities among the country's ethnic minorities. She had so impressed the embassy's deputy chief of mission, he'd run interference to get her a coveted desk officer job, which would prepare her for more senior assignments outside the consular area; and, this was her dream.

A conscientious person; typical of her Wisconsin Protestant upbringing; she threw herself fully into the job, often working late into the evening, surpassing even some of the workaholics who routinely stayed in the office until past six to show how 'hard' they were working. In her case, she actually worked.

A detail oriented person, she often noticed the small things that others missed; thus, when she noticed a small item, only a few sentences really, in the intelligence digest prepared by the department's Bureau of Intelligence and Research, or INR, about the killing of two Dagastani government officials with the suggestion that foreign elements might have been involved, and then, after crosschecking, discovered that the embassy hadn't reported anything on it, she sprang into action. First, she drafted a cable to the embassy, for the political counselor, asking for any information the embassy had on the incident, and its assessment of the impact it would have on

Dagastani politics. Not wanting to bother the office secretary, a sour faced civil servant who liked to remind the young desk officers that she worked for the country director, not them, she'd prepared the cable herself, requiring the typing on a cumbersome multi-copy form of ten green sheets with carbons interlaced, requiring that each sheet be dealt with to make corrections. For that reason, she kept the message short; tactful, but brief. It was when she'd taken it to James Whitman, the country director for that region that sat on the border between Europe and Asia, that her troubles began.

As soon as Whitman had finished reading, he put the paper on his desk, pushing it away as if it was a dangerous animal; and frowning up at her.

"Just what is the meaning of this, Lesley?" he asked. His New England accent, not quite British, but close, was cold, as was his expression.

"Uh, well, sir," she said. "I saw a report about this in the intel traffic. I noticed that the embassy hadn't reported it, but, because of the implication that there might be foreign involvement, I thought they should look into it."

Whitman's expression got even colder. "You thought they should look into it? And, just what makes you think you have any business telling the embassy what they should be doing? Ambassador Ellingsworth is a capable Foreign Service Officer, and if he hasn't reported what is no doubt a minor incident, I'm sure he has his reason, and it's not for a mere desk officer to question him. Do I make myself clear?"

Lesley felt like crying, but held back the tears. She knew he'd expect her to do that. Whitman was one of the people who'd objected to her assignment, stating that a woman, and a consular officer at that, didn't have the necessary qualifications to perform well in the high stress environment of the country directorate. That had been, Lesley find out early on, total bullshit. While they worked often insane hours due to the time difference between Washington and most of the embassies with which they worked, the stress level was less than having to deal with a plane crash or a missing American whose relatives in the U.S. were constantly on the phone insisting that the U.S. Government find their kin, things that even the most junior consular officers had to learn to deal with very early in their careers. The desk officers read cables, wrote bullshit instruction cables, and wrote or cleared on even more bullshit memos for the various senior officials on the sixth and seventh floor of the State Department's C Street headquarters.

This, she thought, should have been just another routine request for additional information. The frosty look on Whitman's face, though, told her it was anything but. She'd done enough time behind visa interview windows, querying foreigners seeking visas to the United States, that she could spot deception with her eyes closed. Whitman was concealing worry; no, she thought; fear; behind his expression of frosty superiority. As he tore the green sheets, carbons included, into pieces and dumped them into the brown paper bag at the corner of his desk, the 'burn' bag into which classified trash was placed for incineration; she noticed that his hands trembled ever so slightly.

Something about the incident bothered him. Lesley Carter was determined to find out what, but decided not to press the issue with him.

"Yes, sir," she said, trying to put a tone of meek submission into her voice. "I just thought it might be useful, but, I see your point."

He nodded, looking at her from beneath his bushy brows. "Very well then; you have more important things to do, so I suggest you get to them. Where, for instance is that analysis of the crop production reports I asked for this morning."

"Uh, it's almost completed. I'll have it for you first thing in the morning."

This meant, she knew, that she'd have to take the files home and would be up all night drafting and redrafting. She'd been working on it intermittently for most of the day, taking the occasional break to read items in the thick read file that circulated through the warren of tiny boxes that passed for office space for the half dozen desk officers she worked with. When she'd come across the intelligence report, it had piqued her interest; here at last was something besides boring columns of figures enumerating the hectares of wheat and other grains produced by the large state farms of Dagastan, outputs that were barely enough to feed its small population, requiring large shipments of grain and other foodstuffs from the country's Russian neighbors.

Dejected and disappointed by Whitman's reaction to her initiative to do something interesting, and to work on something that might actually have some political impact on U.S. relations with the tiny, insignificant country, she turned and with shoulders slumped, headed back to her tiny space; little more than a broom closet in comparison to the large corner office Whitman occupied.

She would have been even more dismayed had she seen Whitman reach for the phone as she left; his narrowed eyes on her retreating back.

Back in her little cubbyhole, Lesley took the carbon copy of the cable Whitman had so casually dismissed and started to crumple it up to put in the burn bag. Then, she hesitated, looking at the purplish type on the green paper.

"No, dammit," she said quietly. "There's something here, and I'm getting to the bottom of it, one way or another."

She carefully smoothed out the single sheet and folded it in thirds. She put the folded paper in a legal size envelope, folded it in half and stuck it in her purse. Technically, she was about to commit a serious security violation, because, as was practice, she'd classified the cable CONFIDENTIAL, but she was so angry at the way she'd been rebuffed, she decided, to hell with it. No one checked employee purses on the way in or out of the State Department, and she could always burn it later.

She then took a sheet of plain paper and in her precise handwriting, wrote a short note. She folded the paper in half taped it, then put it in one of the brown interoffice envelopes used to ferry documents around the warren of hallways of the Department. Addressing the envelope to Alison Chambers, Central Asia Analyst, INR/EUR, she got up and went outside. The secretary was bent over her desk, reading the Washington Post, and paid her no attention as she slipped the envelope into the stack of outgoing interoffice mail.

Back in her office, she spent the rest of the day

making notations on the report Whitman had demanded. She was almost cheered up by the fact that she might actually be able to get most of it down before leaving for the day, alleviating the need to spend all night working on the damn thing.

When the hands of the circular clock mounted on the corkboard wall of her office were at six-fifteen, she removed the ribbon from her typewriter and locked it in the single drawer safe behind her chair, cleared her inbox of all papers, grabbed her purse, and, without looking around to see if anyone was noticing, left for the day. She had no doubt that some, if not all, the desk officers, all male, were sitting hunched over their desks watching the clock, waiting for a suitable 'late' hour to depart. She figured one or more of them would be making a mental note of her 'early' departure. The eight-to-five announced workday was a joke throughout the building. Only the civil servants who had permanent tenure could afford to actually work an eight-hour day.

To hell with it, she thought. The annual performance evaluations, the EERs, had already been done for the year, and she hadn't been in the section long enough to warrant a rating; she'd gotten a glowing evaluation from her last post, which would stand her in good stead when the summer promotion boards met beginning in June.

She was thinking about her prospect for promotion when the big red, white, and blue Metro bus pulled into the stop with a loud hiss of its air brakes, and the group on the sidewalk surged forward even before passengers getting off at that stop could exit the bus.

In the middle of the mass of people, Lesley managed to get on without being pushed around too much, and, luckily, snagged an inward facing seat near the front. Sitting with her back against the wall, jammed in between a sweaty businessman who smelled of too many martinis with his lunch and an elderly black woman who was reading a dog-eared Bible, she kept her gaze fixed on the scuffed floor of the bus. She didn't notice, therefore, the quick glance she got from the man in black as he made his way past her to the back of the bus, where he stood, holding one of the overhead straps.

The L1 bus made its way up Twenty-third Street, around Washington Circle and onto New Hampshire Avenue, and then northwest on Connecticut toward Woodley Park and the National Zoo. By the mid-way point of the journey, and several stops where people got on, but few got off, the bus was crowded to capacity.

The twenty minute journey to Connecticut Avenue and Calvert Street, Lesley's stop, seemed like an eternity on the crowded vehicle with the smell of sweaty bodies and sweaty clothing assaulting her nostrils. The evening air, even with the mixture of gas fumes from all the cars roaring past on Connecticut, was a relief when she stepped down from the bus and headed up the hill toward the little town house she'd been able to rent a week after arriving in Washington for her assignment. Her air freight had arrived, but she was still waiting for her sea freight shipment, so the place was empty except for a card table and folding chair that did duty as dining surface and work space, and a futon upon which she slept. The few books she'd included in her limited air freight shipment were stacked neatly on the floor next to the futon, beside a gooseneck lamp she'd bought at a little shop in Bethesda. She hadn't bought a TV, so when she didn't spend the time before bed reading, she listened to a little transistor radio that her cousin had given her for her thirtieth birthday the previous year.

She was looking forward to getting inside her empty house; empty though it was, it was her territory, and she felt comfortable there, away from the pretense and coldness of official Washington.

She was completely unaware of the man in black, who had exited via the center door when she went out through the front, and was now trailing her, about twenty feet back. The sidewalk was deserted but for the two of them, and even at seven, the sky was still too light for the street lights to be turned on. Towering trees cast islands of deep shadow across the sidewalk. The man stayed as much in the shadows as possible, but it wasn't necessary, Lesley's attention was focused in front of her, and her destination, about half a mile farther along.

The dark stranger used the pools of shadow to close the gap between them, and it was only when he was no more than six feet behind her that Lesley Carter became aware of someone near; it was a feeling of sorts, the kind of itching tingle at the base of your neck that tells you that you're no longer alone. At first, she merely increased her pace. Only another hundred yards or so to go, and she would be inside her house; not, she thought, that she should really have anything to worry about. After all, Woodley Park was a nice area, populated by middle class families and professionals; not at all like some of the other DC neighborhoods where it was unsafe to wander out alone at night. It was probably just a neighbor, like her, coming home from a day of toil in some government office downtown.

It was after she'd made the turn up the side street on which her house stood that she began to have second thoughts about the sound of the footfalls behind her. They'd turned into the tree-lined narrow street that ended in a cul de sac three houses beyond hers moments after she had. She didn't know any of her neighbors, but couldn't recall any of them who would be coming from downtown at this time of day. Most were elderly retired couples who spent all day sitting on their porches or working in their tiny gardens.

She walked faster. Her house was now in sight, but the sidewalk, a dark gray blur in the shadows of the overhanging trees, seemed to stretch on forever. Her heart began to race, pounding in her chest like the native drums she'd heard during her visits to villages in Senegal. She clutched her purse against her small breasts and lowered her head. Could it be, she asked herself, a mugger? One of the lowlifes that infested the downtown areas, including the National Mall, preying on unwary tourists? If so, why was he so far out from town? She thought of the document in the folded envelope in her purse. What if he wanted her purse? Could she perhaps remove the money and placate him, thus not risking the incriminating document accidentally falling into the wrong hands?

The sound of the footsteps behind her was getting closer. Lesley wanted to run, but knew that her short, stocky legs weren't up to it. Suddenly, she felt the heat of anger and stopped in her tracks. The sound of footsteps stopped as well.

She turned slowly, glaring at the surprised man who had followed her from the bus stop. Her heart was pounding. She took a deep breath to try and keep her fear from showing in her voice. "Why are you following me?" she demanded.

The dark figure smiled; a slight upturn of the corners of the slit that was his mouth. The close set eyes bored through her, sending chills coursing throughout her body. She clutched the purse closer to her body.

Slowly, ever so slowly, as if he had all the time in the world, the figure advanced. He had his right hand in his pocket, the left hanging loosely at his side.

"If it's money you want," Lesley said. A bit of panic was creeping into her trembling voice. "You can have it; just leave me alone."

The man, who stood less than an inch taller than her five-eight, but who had broader shoulders and a narrow waist, was now less than arms' length away. She could smell the musky cologne he wore. His smile broadened, showing gleaming white teeth.

Something deep in her lizard brain told Lesley that this was no ordinary mugging. She began to take a step backwards, still holding the purse against her chest.

The stranger's hand came out of the pocket and darted forward. Lesley got only a glimpse of the glittering length of steel before she felt the hot piercing in her chest just above her hands clasping the purse.

At first, it was as if someone had touched her flesh with a hot ember, a burning sensation that seemed to spread from the dark man's hand which seemed to be resting between her small breasts. She tried to will her legs to move, to back away from his too familiar touch, but they wouldn't respond. Then, the heat was replaced with an intense feeling of cold that seemed to radiate outward from his hand to all parts of her body.

Slowly, she was immersed in a mixed web of feeling, fire lanced through her chest, and she could feel warmth flowing down over her abdomen; at the same time, she felt cold, oh, so cold. Her vision began to blur, and it was as if she was floating in the air some feet above herself, looking down at her body as it began to slowly crumple toward the sidewalk.

As she lay on the rough concrete, a pool of her blood spreading out around her, the light slowly fading from her eyes, the stranger knelt and removed the purse from her clutching fingers. Smiling, he stood, looking down at her with no other emotion.

He stood there until the erratic rise and fall of her chest had stopped and the life had completely gone from her eyes. Then, he turned and walked back the way he'd come. After turning onto Calvert, he stopped and opened the purse, removing the folded envelope and stuffing it in his left pants' pocket. He then tossed the purse into the foliage and continued walking toward Connecticut Avenue, whistling softly to himself.

About the Author

Charles Ray has been writing fiction since his teens, winning a national Sunday school magazine writing contest while still in junior high school. He has worked as a newspaper and magazine journalist during the 60s and 70s, contributing articles, reviews, photographs, and artwork to publications in the US and abroad. His first full length work was a book on leadership, *Things I Learned from My Grandmother About Leadership and Life*, published in 2008. In 2009, he began writing fiction again, with the first in the Al Pennyback mystery series, *Color Me Dead*. He has since published more than 30 works of fiction and non-fiction.

A native of Texas who now calls Maryland home, he served 20 years in the army, and upon retirement joined the US Foreign Service, serving as a diplomat in more than six countries, and dealing with scores of others. Since his retirement from public service in 2012, he has devoted most of his time to writing and public speaking.

For more information on his published works, check his author page at: http://www.amazon.com/Charles-Ray/e/B006WMLEZK or follow his tweets at http://www.twitter.com/charlieray45.